5ᵀᴴ AND VANGUARD
LEE ADAMS

The year is 1999.

I'm perched atop the hood of one of the used cars in Munson's lot talking into a small tape recorder and staring at the intersecting signs across the street. That's the corner, 5th and Vanguard. That's the liquor store I was standing in front of a couple of months ago thinking how stupid it was for a girl to be out so late, for anybody really. But I couldn't sleep that night so I took a walk.

The biography I'm compiling now will be the first thing I've written in almost three years, a combination of self-loathing and sobriety having frightened away my muse. Seems she was tied up with a drug habit of mine and once I conquered it, I lost her, as well. That's the way I've rationalized it, anyway.

But sometimes second chances are issued without solicitation and without being earned. Circumstance can turn on a dime, which is what happened to me in front of that liquor store on that corner.

That night, as I had for several nights, I'd taken a walk in pursuit of something nameless that wouldn't let me sleep. And whatever it was, I was ready to confront it somewhere on the concrete streets of Berle, my hometown.

Berle is not the most picturesque of all seaside communities. It's a little beat up. It's a little moldy from the constant sea breeze that salts its perimeters.

Originally designed as an upper-class oceanfront resort catering to tourists, celebrities and the privileged few, it ended up housing a very blue-collar population. Close enough to L.A. to mimic its cosmopolitan swagger and far enough away to remain modestly unaffected, we do own bowling shirts but we actually bowl in them.

Still, our boardwalk and beach continue to bring in tourists and there's a great deal of old money up in the hills, money and mansions. I don't get up there much. I spend most of my time in the poshless utilitarianism of downtown Berle. That's where I inevitably end up on my late night walks, usually in front of the squinting fluorescence of a liquor store called Bob's Liquor Palace, open all night.

The weather goosed me into involuntary aerobics as I stood huddled and pulling on a bottle of Orange Crush in front of a Bohemia beer poster taped to the inside of the glass. I buttoned the collar of my army surplus coat and leaned against the stucco, contemplating nothing heavier than why I was standing there freezing when I could be in my warm little house. Then a vague sense of uneasiness came over me. It was the same feeling I'd had for the past several nights whenever I tried to go to sleep, but this time I was wide-awake and it was much worse.

Looking through the naked glass between the beer poster and a lottery sign, I checked on Sandy, the liquor store clerk. He was standing behind the counter like he was supposed to be.

Despite that reassurance, something close to panic started to creep into my consciousness and I began to sweat. The rusted Pall Mall thermometer nailed to Bob's plaster storefront read 49°, and I was sweating. I checked my watch as if I needed to know the time. It was about 3 A.M.

Feeling faint, I threw the pop bottle into a dented trashcan chained to the sidewalk then clutched both cold metal sides for balance. While trying to regroup I noticed something on my hands, something like syrup or dark oil. Letting go of the dirty aluminum, I rolled my fingers over each palm trying to rub off the foul stuff to determine what it was that I'd gotten into. Then, all at once, I knew exactly what it was. It was blood.

I gasped, reflexively dragging both hands against my coat several times before cautiously taking another look. There wasn't anything on my hands. Nothing at all.

I stared at both clean palms for a moment trying to figure out what had just happened then grabbed the can again, unburdening my stomach onto a half-eaten burrito at the bottom. I thought how I really

4

ought to look into one of those sleep clinics you hear about on the radio.

That's when the Cadillac pulled up. My brain spun like hot sugar in a cotton candy machine but my feet remained planted between the trashcan and streetlight as I stared at the couple emerging. A calm centeredness came over me. The sweats subsided.

She got out of the backseat, this macabre, stylish old woman. I had the strong sense that I knew her, that I'd seen her get out of a million backseats before.

Even with the dark lipstick and rouge she had an almost regal quality about her, like a silent movie queen. Small framed and short in stature, she somehow managed to appear imposing. Her face was lineless and waxy giving the impression of a well-constructed mask, yet her advanced age peeked through. Could've been the way she carried herself, almost mechanically. Looked like it hurt. Looked like her feelings had been hurt, as well.

She was wearing sunglasses. At 3 A.M. this should have read like quite a pretentious prop but it didn't. I fantasized that she was hiding something, maybe a black eye or unsavory intentions. Her nose pinched every few seconds like something smelled bad. For no particular reason I was beginning to agree.

Then an old man got out of the driver's seat and hurried around the Cadillac while she steadied herself, shaking her head at the wind. When I tell you he looked like the shadow of a man, I don't mean frail. I mean he looked like a shadow, featureless under the brim of that cool yet dated hat, as if he had a stocking pulled over his face but there was no stocking. He threw his arm around her waist and escorted her into

Bob's Liquor Palace. They didn't pay any attention to me. Not yet.

I lit a cigarette. Glancing up and down the street, I observed that we were very much alone here, me and that huge, black, 1955 Cadillac. You would've sworn it was brand new. The thing was so sure of itself, it made me and the liquor store look painfully underdressed.

Damp burgundy locks blew loose around my beret and corrective lenses as I stepped closer to have a look inside. Beautiful. Everything original and clean as a whistle. No cigarette wrappers or coffee cups cluttering the showroom tuck-and-roll, just a red chiffon scarf on the backseat, and a little gun next to it. I stood rapt for longer than is probably prudent when your object of interest is a gun. Pretty sloppy leaving it there, I thought.

I had an impulse to check on Sandy again, though I wasn't sure what I could do to help him even if he needed it. They sure didn't look like thieves. Still, a gun, though unable to hurt anyone from where it was, marked these two as suspicious and worthy of closer observation.

I slowly moved away from the car and toward the liquor store, but before I got there they came flying out the door in tandem. Her short wool cape picked up behind her in the wind making her look like some kind of comic book hero, or villain, and she was clutching something close to her chest.

The shadow opened the door for her then jogged around the Cad, jumped back into the driver's seat, and waited for her to get in. She stopped short as if she wasn't in a hurry at all, and looked right at me. Her dark lenses reflected my naive expression back my way. I could literally see myself through her eyes.

In that silence, we had a little conversation. Me: "What's going on? Do I know you?" Her: "Who are you, poor darling? What are you doing out this late?" The shadow barked from behind the steering wheel, "Max!"

She responded by folding herself into the car as the engine raced idle. The window was down. Five fake nails and one real diamond gleamed in the amber glow from the streetlight above. She pulled herself to the window frame with that useless-looking hand, trying to turn and look at me. From her vantage point I was hard to see, and I wasn't moving. Giving up (it was only a half-assed gesture anyway), she arranged herself against the upholstery and dropped the gun out the window as the car sped away.

Seemed she wanted me to take it for some reason. Protection? Evidence? So I'd be the jerk smearing fingerprints on it as the cops pulled up? I stared at it. Then, in that smart has never been one of my strong suits, I moved toward it.

I remember thinking this was the prettiest gun I'd ever seen, though I'd never actually seen one before. Looked no worse for the fall. Such a pretty thing, real shiny, even had rhinestones around the little handle. When I picked it up I noticed it didn't have any weight to it. I poked at the chamber with the tip of my index finger. No bullets. Butane. It was a lighter.

Flicking my smoke into the gutter, I slid my shiny new toy into an inside pocket of my peacoat for safekeeping. Lovely gift. Maybe she decided I'd seen it and wanted me to know it wasn't a gun, in case anyone asked. Or maybe she just quit smoking. I turned from the street and faced the glass door I'd passed through on so many occasions.

Sandy was behind the counter as usual. That's all that was usual about it. He was propped up against the wall facing the walk-in humidor. Hands behind his back, typical duct-tape-over-the-mouth bit like you see in the movies. I couldn't believe that someone I saw every day was right in front of me bound and gagged. They had worked fast.

I wanted to help him but just stood there rubbing my hands and cursing loudly. "Shit. Oh, shit, man. Oh, God." His eyes suggested that I get over it and untape him. Shaking, I complied.

The duct tape came off his sleeves easily enough. Hadn't been taped all that well. His mouth was another story. I let him do it.

"Thanks. Damn." Sandy rubbed the back of his head then checked his fingers for blood.

"Maybe you hit it on the way down."

"Yeah. Lucky you were still hanging around."

He spoke in a thin, breathless voice still looking at the sliding glass of the humidor propped open by a box of cigars that had fallen in the tussle. Her perfume lingered in the refrigerated air.

Sandy wasn't the fastest horse in the race and a little rough around the edges, even for me. His hair was long. He could've showered more. Everything he wore seemed somehow wrong, nylon blends straining over steroid muscles. But he was likable in an oafish way.

We only knew each other within the context of my liquor store transactions but had always made time for a little extra chitty chat while I was there.

I suppose on some abstract level, I was fond of

Sandy, fond of his worthlessness cloaked in bravado, his brutishness, his fragility. His large water-blue
eyes were both sweet and dangerous, a fine combination in a man. In the brief conversations we shared,
he always looked like a Neanderthal staring at fire,
wide-eyed, wrinkled brow. Maybe it wasn't fond-
ness. Maybe it was pity.

Anyway, none of these thoughts about Sander
Harper had been exhumed before that evening. The
idea of sharing anything profound with Sandy, even
an extended conversation, well, I just wouldn't have
guessed it. But Fate had plans for us that night, and a
wicked sense of humor.

"What was that, for God's sake? What did they do
to you? You okay?" I was petting his head like that
might help.

"Nothing. Nothing, Julie." He finally looked at
me, seeming to shake off the fog that had rendered
him dumb. Then he got us both to our feet. "I think
you better go now. I'm all right. That was weird.
Thanks again, Julie."

He was starting to scare me.

"That was weird? What are you talking about?
I'm calling the cops."

"No, don't." Sandy slapped his hand over the receiver just after I'd done the same. We were nose-
to-nose.

Releasing the phone, I repositioned myself a
step back from him. He folded his arms and leaned
against the register drawer looking down. I broke the
awkward silence.

"What's going on here? What did she want?"

His internal monologue tumbled out. "No fucking way am I calling the cops. That's all I need." He

guffawed under his breath, "Like they could help me with this shit." Then he remembered I was still standing across from him. "Look, Julie, nobody got shot, okay? I'm fine. Forget it. Can you do that? Just forget it. It was nothing."

"Nothing? I don't know, man. It was something. What's the matter with you?"

"Nothing. It's good, okay?"

I stared at him.

Realizing he had to cough up something, he bought time by opening a carton of Viceroys and stacking individual packs alongside the Vantage and Salem. While he stocked, he stammered, "I...I don't even know how to tell it to you. I don't know what's going on exactly. They walked up to the counter. I said 'can I help you' and the little guy says... he says..."

Sandy trailed off, lost in the instant replay rolling through his gummy head. I gave him a push.

"Go on, Sandy. What did they want?"

"A box of cigars. A special box. One that I was holding for someone." He threw the empty carton away shooting me a pained expression. "Jeez. You want some coffee? I could really do with a cup of coffee."

"I'll get it."

I went around the corner toward the coffeepots as Sandy straightened out the silk-screened wolf head on the front of his black jersey shirt. Unfortunately, the only pot steaming was housing a vanilla walnut blend.

"Here." I handed him a Styrofoam cup. "So exactly how big is this cesspool you're wading in?"

"I don't know. Christ. A couple of days ago, a guy comes in here. Asks me if I want to make a little easy money. I'm shaking my head, like, no way but I'm saying, like, 'How?' and 'Who I gotta kill?' and shit. God, this coffee sucks."

He paused, looking to me for my opinion, which I offered. "Yes, it does." He took another drink and continued.

"So he says a guy would be by to pick up something in three days and he's real clear about that, which means tomorrow, describes the guy to me, how he's going to be wearing a red suit and so on and I say, 'That's it?' He says yeah, I just have to be careful to only give this particular red guy the goods. And that's all. And then five hundred clams are in my pocket."

He stopped there, his blue eyes widening as he snorted in astonishment. I think he thought he'd finished the story.

"Sandy?"

"What?"

I waited.

"Oh, so, whatever, they come swooshing in here tonight and the little guy asks for the cigars and I'm freaked out for a second and then I say I've never heard of that cigar, blah, blah, blah."

"And while you're stammering this badly executed lie to Boris, Natasha's burrowing through the humidor, right?"

"You know these people?"

I took a breath and tried again. "What happened after that?"

"Okay, so then, when I start to go after her, he grabs my shirt, pulls me close, and puts some kind of Vulcan death grip on me. Real calmly pinches my neck and good night, Irene."

"Even money says the cigars are gone," I said as we both moved into the humidor to look for the missing product. "Red suit. What kind of guy has a red suit?"

Oblivious to the insult, Sandy idly added, "I got a red suit."

I walked into that. "Oh. Well, I'll bet it's real nice. So, what are we looking for in here?"

"They're called Montego Supremes. Only, it's a joke. There's no such thing. Hot looking box, though. Unless you knew better, you wouldn't know."

"How do you know?"

"Some things I know."

"Probably weren't cigars at all, right?"

"Hell, I don't know. Yeah, it's fucking gone. It's mother! fucking! gone!"

He threw punches with each word. When he finished pummeling the box of cigars nearest his fist, I made a suggestion.

"More coffee?"

While allowing his breathing to become regular again, he nodded affirmatively. We stepped back into the store proper as he pulled the glass door closed behind us. I refilled his cup.

"Did the goon with the $500 proposition tell you they were fakes?"

He took a gulp, set the Styrofoam next to the empty hotdog steamer, crossed his arms across his huge chest, and leaned in toward my ear like he was going to tell me a secret. "Look, Julie, I don't know what's supposed to happen next but I really think you should get away from here. Maybe everything is okay but I don't know. I could've fucked up real big this time."

I stayed put and whispered back, "What are you going to do?"

"I don't know."

By the expression on his wide face, I knew that was the truth. He had no idea what to do. Though I viewed the whole thing as some great riddle, he seemed to be taking it very hard.

I harnessed my critical thinking skills to deduce what might happen next on my own. The obvious thing would be for the guy in the red suit to drop by, realize that the box had been pilfered and then, what, break Sandy's knees? In that I wasn't terribly familiar with these situations, I really couldn't guess at the ramifications. But Sandy knew what might happen. That's why he was so concerned.

"Sandy, that guy gave you the money already?"

"Yeah. Look, Julie, I know this must sound real strange and all but sometimes illegal cigars come through here if there's a demand, and there usually is, and if the price is right I fence 'em. They always need some fence. This deal didn't seem that weird to me at the time. Guess I was wrong."

"I guess. So, why the fake box?"

Sandy rubbed his bruised noggin.

"You must've figured this was more than cigar smuggling. Cigar smuggling wouldn't require some elaborate fake box, would it? I mean, it would be easier to move something in a box more recognizable anyway, right? And why give you the money up front? Unless…Sandy, you know the guy who gave you the money, don't you?" I delivered that last question as a statement.

He took on this horrible expression. I convinced myself it was somebody else's life that shot across his now unfamiliar face. Then he made a choking sound like he was about to cry, grabbed me by the shoulders, and shook me hard enough to open my sinuses.

"Get the fuck out of here. Don't come back and don't say nothing about any of this shit to no one – ever. Do you get that, Julie? Do you understand exactly what I'm saying to you?"

My neck snapped back and forth as he squeezed the air out of me. It hadn't sunk in until right then that I might be in any danger. That this clerk I'd seen and spoken to a million times might actually harm me. Hell, he could kill me. But even as my glasses bounced up and down off the bridge of my nose, I couldn't believe it, not Sandy.

"Stop it. Jesus Christ, Sandy, let me go."

His jaw unclenched nominally considering his options as I considered mine. My heart was beating like a rabbit's but I had to take action before the big ox inadvertently dislocated my shoulder.

"I…I'm just...Sandy, I care about you."

His hands remained wrapped around my arms but the pressure in them dissipated. "Aw, me too, Julie. I care about you, too. I don't know what I'm gonna do. You don't fuck with these people." He pressed his chin against the top of my head. "Shit. I think I'm in big trouble."

"Sandy, who are you talking about? Tell me the truth this time. Maybe I can help you."

His hands were like c-clamps on either side of me as his eyes searched the magazine rack then cupcake display for advice that didn't come. I decided to change my tack.

"Look, maybe it's time for you to take a little vacation."

"Oh, yeah, I could really do with a vacation about now."

"No. I mean maybe you should hop on your bike and get lost for a few days."

You could see by the way his eyes punctured mine that he hadn't thought of it. There was hope in this fresh idea.

"Yeah, I could leave town."

"Yeah. Or, you know, call the cops."

He started shaking me again. A very clear non-verbal shut up about the cops. This time I yelled. Then he started yelling, nearly lifting me off the ground. My glasses flew in one direction, my beret in the other.

"Shit, Julie, I need the money! I really need this job with these people. Guys like me don't get opportunities like this too fucking much. I don't know. Maybe I'm a dead man. Oh, shit, I'm a dead man."

In my panic, some survival instinct kicked in and a series of random, empty affirmations flew from my lips as if I was trying to crack the combination to a safe with words.

"Calm down. We can fix it. It's not too late. It's not your fault. I'm your friend. You can trust me."

He stopped. I tried that number again.

"Sandy? Sandy, you do trust me, don't you?"

And with that, the door to the safe fell open. Every muscle in him relaxed. Then the poor fool threw his big paws around me and gave me a hug, convinced that he could trust me. He was wrong. He couldn't, not after that little display. I didn't necessarily want to see him in any trouble but between beating that cigar box and shaking me like a clogged ketchup bottle, I knew this was not someone I should be hanging out with.

"I'm sorry, Julie. I didn't hurt you, did I? Sometimes I don't know my own strength," he admitted while retrieving my fallen glasses and hat and handing them back.

"It's okay, Sandy." I forced myself to smile sympathetically.

I felt kind of shitty lying to him but playing the "you can trust me" card was a simple knee-jerk reaction. Be charming. Make like everything's cool. Things were far from cool. For all I knew, if he wasn't about to get killed he was about to kill somebody else. Whatever it was, it wasn't good.

Still, I was invigorated in a way I had not been in a long time, alert and focused. My arms were throbbing from the abuse they'd taken but I still didn't want to leave. I wanted to solve this little mystery more than I wanted to sleep, more than I wanted to write. All of a sudden, solving it meant more than anything. And I was nearly giddy thinking that if I did, it might turn out to be really big and messy, maybe even dangerous.

Self-preservation was no match for the burgeoning sense that something very real had presented itself to me. My late night walks were about to pay off.

2

We stood inches from one another, both exhausted, both flush with adrenaline.

"What if I don't ever see you again? What if this is it?"

"Look, I'm sure you're over-reacting, Sandy. Just tell me who she is and we'll figure this out."

Once again he looked like he was about to cry, but instead, swallowed hard and seized the moment. His hot breath wetted my glasses before his lips made a crash landing on mine. There was no finesse about it. It was primal. A resounding kiss, like maybe he thought he wouldn't get a chance to kiss anybody for a long time.

I shifted in an effort to move my mouth away but he found it with his own, thrusting that huge tongue further inside me than is convenient while kissing. I curbed a gag reflex. Acquiescing, however distasteful, would buy me time and time was paramount if I was going to pry more information from him. Besides, it was Sandy. If I could work around his violent side, surely I could handle this.

"Okay, that's enough," I whispered. "You're just scared."

"I got nobody, man. Nobody. They could throw me in the fucking desert and nobody would come looking, you know? I am scared, Julie. I'm really fucking scared."

I was getting a little scared myself. It was then that I decided things had gone far enough. "Okay, you need to let me go now. Right now."

He froze. All at once he was seven and I was the second grade teacher. Then someone grunted near the door. Thankfully, we were no longer alone.

"Sander! Sander, where the hell are you?" This grinding train wreck of a voice broke Sandy's concentration. We turned to face our chaperone who had just then turned to face us.

"Whoa, Sandy, is that your beach? Ha!"

Sandy wiped his mouth and made busy by going over to turn the light out in the humidor.

"Carroll, my favorite drunk. What are you doing here, man? Bar closed hours ago."

"Did it? Well, where the hell have I been?"

The guy lunged toward the counter for balance proceeding to straighten individual Juicy Fruits and Dentynes in their boxes. He wore a threadbare baby blue polyester suit under an unbuttoned thrift-store trench coat with a gray sock safety pinned around his skinny neck in lieu of a scarf. Looked to be in his late fifties, early sixties. Hard to tell. The bags under his tiny eyes were twice as big as the eyes themselves and his nose, a road map of broken blue veins and deep black pores.

"Hello."

He was talking to me. "Hi."

Unfortunately, this drunk had done more than break up an improbable, wayward kiss. He had forced my hand. I couldn't ask any more questions and I shouldn't really come back if I was smart. Made it hard to leave, so I stood there hugging myself in the absence of more commanding arms.

"Look, Carroll, you stumbled in here on kind of a freak night, dude. I was just about to close shop. What can I do you for?"

What if Sandy had decided to hit the road after all? Whether those old folks were foreign spies or just some aunt and uncle he didn't want to own up to, the answer would go with him. I couldn't let that happen. Everything I wanted to know was sitting nearly visible right behind those vacant eyes. That's one of the sweet things about the simple-minded. They don't keep secrets very well.

"Son, I didn't just stumble in here. No sir, this is where I belong. Drunks and liquor stores keep each other motivated. That's my opinion. A relationship that quite simply works. No dootabootit."

Sandy glanced at me from behind the counter making a subtle nod toward the door but I wanted to know more about cigar fencing and the drunk wanted liquor.

"How 'bout a little something, oh, let me see, a little pint of, I don't know, maybe a little Kahlua. I'm a kidder. How 'bout that Cutty right there? So, why are we closing a 24-hour shop for the night again? You and this nice lady got plans?"

Sandy rang up the scotch quickly, bagged it, and then took the guy's wallet fishing out enough money to cover the purchase. An odd courtesy extended in a perfectly natural way. Led me to believe this was their regular routine.

"Oh, well, we've got a health inspector coming

in here in a couple hours. I want to get everything cleaned up real good."

"Health inspector?" Carroll's tiny eyes swirled around like glass swizzle sticks from his red vinyl face. He obviously didn't buy it. "Did you say health inspector, Sander?"

"That's what I said." And apparently, that's what he was going to stand by without revision. "See you tomorrow."

Carroll turned to me while unscrewing his bottle cap. "Let me guess. You're a waitress. Am I right? I've got a real flair for this sort of thing. Wait. No, I was right the first time, definitely waitress. Okay, I give. What kind of work you do again?"

Sandy gave me a more overt nod to scram while fiddling with the cash.

"Come on now, um, Carroll."

I was urging him out, holding the door open for the both of us. He stood tall by the Cup O'Noodles clearly not ready to go.

"You're getting kind of chummy there, aren't you, missy? Not that I mind, mind you. What's your name, again?" He took a step toward me. "What kind of work you say you do?"

Sandy was counting on me. "Writer. I'm a writer." That always works. Indeed, Carroll was on my heels and my heels were on the sidewalk.

"Hey, me, too. I'm a writer, too."

"No, man, you're a story," I muttered under my breath. "Take care, Sandy," I shouted through the glass.

"Okay, Doris." Sandy shouted back, barely looking up from counting the money as he called me Doris.

That was it. That was the last time I saw Sander Harper. My last memory of him to this day is of him calling me Doris. I'm thinking he didn't want Carroll to know my real name. One way to distance me from any forthcoming monkey business, I suppose. It was decent of him. Silly, but decent.

I turned left onto Vanguard pissed that I hadn't plucked the information I wanted from that big, doughy head.

Carroll tried to keep up with me but he was, you know, drunk. I carried on, readjusting my beret and specs, pulling my coat collar tight around me.

Carroll bellowed between gasps for air, "The air bit like a... like a mad dog as she... pulled her... felt cliché down over icy ears."

He was attempting to prove that he really was a writer. I recognized the desperation. It was almost touching. He stopped trying to keep up with me in front of The Cat's Meow, a local watering hole of zero renown. It was a logical place for him to stop even though the doors were locked for the night. As I moved further away, he called after me, "Hey, can we do this again some time?"

I passed all the usual places on my way home, Willie's Tin Shop, the old Duchess Typewriter Repair, but nothing looked right. One of the neon hearts in the window of Valentine's Bakery had accidentally been left on, its soft pink light illuminating the cracked pavement beneath me. I had to leap off of the curb and into the street to escape a fire hydrant that blew just as I passed. My head hurt.

If I went to the cops, what could I tell them? That an over-dressed woman and featureless man stole a box of cigars? Would I save Sandy's life by having the cops case the place or would I get him killed? Should I give a shit?

By the time I hit Poppy my feet and thoughts were flying. That old woman definitely looked me square in the eye. Surely, she could identify me.

Once inside the house I turned the deadbolt and drew the chain, leaning against the wood and breathing hard. That fire hydrant blowing provided the perfect final note to the wildest night I'd had since being sober. Ugly thrills, like playing tag with the devil. I wasn't even sure who won.

3

❖❖❖❖❖❖

First thing that I saw upon prying my face from the door was Felix in his underwear asleep where I'd left him in a semi-upright position on the couch. Earlier that evening he'd spilled barbecue sauce on both his T-shirt and boxers while trying to eat chicken from a cheap paper plate. His mouth was open. Looked like he'd been shot.

Felix Mint and I have been living together for three years now. While I was drying out, physically and artistically, I used to walk all the way across town to LaRue's to hear him play the saxophone, this brilliant brooding musician with coal-black, Eraserhead hair and a wardrobe so ridiculous you knew when you saw him he was a man of great courage.

I've always been weak for genius and he has it, an intoxicating brilliance. His bass-heavy Brooklyn accent might betray his intelligence but the magic that cascades from his horn sets the story straight. The first time I saw him play, I knew that this subterranean demigod had been handpicked and sent up from Coolsville to heal my self-inflicted wounds. He possessed all the bravado I lacked, all the possibility I had destroyed.

I'd sit there drinking coffee into the wee hours trying to figure out how to get that tall drink of water over to my table. Eventually I discovered that by buying him a drink he would come right over. Soon, he came over without the bribe. Everything about Felix is so easy. We couldn't be more different.

As I looked at him sprawled out on the couch, I thought about waking him so he could do the rest of his sleeping in a bed but chose to let him be.

He'd been working on this high-dollar project that had him rolling in at dawn and sleeping until it was time to go back in the studio. But he'd had that day off and the poor daddy couldn't even get it up to finish his chicken.

It was pushing 5:00. I took a long shower while trying to decide whether or not I was going to work. In the sanctuary of the steam, I tried to pragmatically consider the events that had just transpired. Was I making more of my visit to the liquor store than necessary? Was I imagining the worst just to entertain myself? No, it all really happened and it wasn't a typical night on the town, but maybe I should leave it alone. It wasn't my responsibility to fix anything or even share it with the cops. I could choose to simply forget it as Sandy had requested. But I didn't want to.

I fumbled with a comb and toothbrush. Yeah, I was going to work. Maybe a day of tedium would put things into perspective. Besides, I had a deadline to hit and sobriety had made me nothing if not dependable. Well, it was more like compulsive and ordered but let's call that dependability.

I shuffled into the kitchen and made a pot of real coffee.

"Baby. Hey now." Felix was behind me sliding his arms around my big old bathrobe and leaning his chin on my neck.

"Time for work. Somebody's gotta work," he murmured as he kissed my cheek prior to bowing before the coffeepot. I poured us both a cup and for one beautiful heartbeat my world consisted of the smell of fresh coffee, the warmth of my chenille robe, and the sound of Felix rubbing his five o'clock shadow.

It occurred to me that Felix didn't think I'd been anywhere but in bed. For all he knew I was just getting up and ready for another day. We sat at the gray linoleum dinette table, sipping, staring.

"Are you working tonight, Felix? I got a story I want to tell you."

"Oh, I love stories."

"Yeah, this is a good one."

His sleep-heavy lids blinked twice around those dark brown marbles as he furrowed his brow.

"It is, huh? Well, I'm going to bed in a minute. Perfect time for a story."

He was so tired and I didn't want to give him an expurgated version.

"No, that's okay. I gotta go to work. But I've had a kind of adventure. And I really need your advice because this is quite a caper."

He chortled, rubbing his crazy black hair. "Caper? Did you seriously just use the word caper?"

"It's a legitimate word."

"Baby, come on. That's completely, like, illegitimate. In three years, you've never used that word."

"Felix, honey, try to let it go. Are you in the studio tonight?"

"It's just funny, that's all. Anyway, when did you fit in a caper?"

I leaned in and quietly asked, "Do you work tonight or not?"

He yawned. "I'm sorry, baby. Yeah, but it starts pretty late, like ten or something. When you get home we'll go down to the coffeehouse and talk out the caper, Nancy Drew. Solid?" He pecked my cheek.

I gave him a peck back. "Thanks."

He downed the coffee and pushed out his chair.

"It's very exciting when you throw new words into the relationship."

In no time, Felix had hit the sack and I, the road. Funny, I wasn't tired. The sky was dark purple. There was no traffic. I arrived at work early for the first time in my life.

A reporter I saw upon entering the paper insisted we stop the presses to headline the fact that I was not only on time but actually early. I couldn't argue the uniqueness of the situation. When I took this job, I was so amazed that they would consider someone with no solid work history as employable that my whole focus had been on keeping it and not fucking up. But being late each morning was the last small vestige of rebellion I'd maintained amidst my new-and-improvedness.

Did I mention I write for a newspaper? I'm no journalist, just the hack who spits out advertising copy for the marketing department. It's better than being unemployed. Back when I was working on the great American novel and stealing pills, I didn't really eat. Now I eat, which requires money.

I've sold cosmetics, been a tour guide, waited tables. The job is the set-up, the paycheck is the punch line. Santa's helper, party clown, envelope stuffer. Now I had a job wherein they let me write. It wasn't Moby Dick I was writing but words were involved and that felt like great progress.

My last employment opportunity saw me selling dead frogs in the East Village. Glazed frogs. You've seen them. Little animated things with plastic bubble eyes forced into adorable positions playing banjos and guitars and such.

There were a number of other distinctive treasures available from that particular boutique but it's the frogs I remember most clearly. It's the frogs that made me so happy to be at the paper. I kept one on my desk as a kind of touchstone. I was looking at it as someone from Human Resources approached.

She stuck a memo in my hand regarding an upcoming 401k meeting. While I tried to digest its content, the weight of the night before and complete lack of sleep began to overwhelm me. My head started swimming in this surreal nightmarish confusion, like, "What am I doing at this desk?" And, "I'm not a gal who has a 401k plan, am I?"

I thought these things while writing the copy for the flyers and rack cards that were waiting in my in-box, because I'm dependable. After that, I cleverly managed to sleep at my desk for the bulk of the day. Eve came over and poked me around 4:30.

Eve is a chatty woman of about sixty. There's something in her obstinate, confrontational manner that I've always enjoyed. She has huge opinions about everything and believes in sharing them. My favorite thing about Eve is that she can maintain a level of controversy where, prior to her two cents, there was none.

"Hey, Julie, either wake up or close your eyes. You're giving me the heebie-jeebies. Listen, there's cake in the third floor conference room. This is Henry's last day. They're throwing him a little party. Come on, kiddo." She considered my condition. "Boy, you and Felix must've either had one hell of a good night or one hell of a bad fight."

I came to, sort of. "God, no Eve. I don't want any cake. But you carry on, good soldier. Go, eat some for me. Who's Henry?"

She sounded like Charlie Brown's mom. "Wa wa, wa wa wa wa wa."

"Eve. I don't really care."

"Oh, for the love of Ike, go home, Julie. Do us all a favor."

She was right. I had to get out of there. Groggy and disoriented, I gathered my things and asked the boss if I could leave early so as to say goodbye to Henry. Luckily, he knew who Henry was. When I hit the pavement, I felt like I'd just cashed in a Get Out Of Jail Free card.

Searching my purse for the car keys, I heard Charlotte calling after me from somewhere down the street. "Char?" I hollered even before locating her.

She was running to greet me (if you can call it running) in a black vinyl mini skirt and ankle-strap stilettos, all 225 pounds of her. The dimples and sponginess that would be evident on a white woman her size go unnoticed against her milk chocolate skin. And besides, between the wigs and shoes, she keeps all the attention where she wants it, whenever she wants it.

Charlotte and I have been friends for as long as I've known Felix and the two of them go way back.

The Charlotte Vaughn Trio has been a staple in Berle's music scene for decades. Her pipes are nearly as well known as Felix's horn, at least locally.

"Girl, move a little. Don't make me run all the way in these heels."

"Sorry, toots," I laughed, walking to meet her.

"Julie, honey, where the hell have you been? I haven't seen you in weeks. Everything cool?"

I stared at her, my mouth still bent in a semi-smile, thinking how much I'd like to talk to her about everything, about not being able to sleep and late night walks. About liquor store clerks and premonitions and the hot rush of thinking I might really be in some kind of danger. I wanted to tell her that I knew something was coming unhinged in me, something that probably shouldn't have been pinned together in the first place, but I just stared, smiling.

"Julie, are you in there?"

"I'm sorry, Char. I'm not sleeping very well these days. Everything's fine. I'm fine. How you doing?"

My pal assessed that assessment with a look of skepticism on her pretty, painted face. "M-hmmm. Yes, you look real good. Felix behaving himself?"

My boyfriend's popular with the ladies.

"Yeah! Yeah. Nothing like that. He'll be sorry he missed you."

She nodded suspiciously. "Well, I've got places to go. I got to get these nails filled before I go to the club tonight."

As she sashayed away, she kept talking. "Let me know when you feel like doing a little shopping. There's a pair of emerald earrings at Saks been calling my name."

"Hey, Charlotte," I said without thinking through

what I was willing to share. She stopped and turned around, clearly ready to listen were I to offer up the dirt but I couldn't. "Nothing. I'll call you."

She pouted her lips and wrinkled her brow. After waiting a beat she gave up and resumed walking. "Door's always open."

The ride home was not like the ride up. Traffic was ridiculous. The lights were all red or broken. I couldn't get the radio dial to stay tuned to any one station. The guy in the car behind me didn't care about my radio. He would honk then flap his arm around like that might propel me forward more quickly. It didn't.

I rolled on pensively sorting out my immediate future. What I couldn't manage to tell Charlotte I would try and tell Felix. If he thought I should call the cops, I would. If not, I wouldn't. But either way, I would not go back to the liquor store nor would I start whining about my nice, steady job. And I'd take walks during my lunch hour, like people do, not at 3:00 A.M. It was settled.

I told myself that whatever went down the night before was Sandy's problem, not mine. Just a mistake, not providence. His adventure, not my adventure.

I was once again alert, even tense, and ever so eager to get home to Felix and a handful of something in capsule form. My sinuses were killing me.

4
◇◇◇◇◇◇◇

As I made my way up Bartelle and over to 163rd, I pulled out the curious gift still tucked away in my coat pocket and lit a cigarette with it. Maybe it was Sandy's adventure but the lighter was mine.

I made a sharp left turn onto Rose and hit the curb in front of B & J's Tool & Die. Funny neighborhood I live in, part industrial park, part residential. Berle houses many such districts. You pass B & J's, then Smith Premium Steel, then a dirt lot and a string of houses before you get to Poppy. Our California bungalow is situated between a rundown Craftsman-style home to one side and a working oil derrick on the other. There's another derrick directly across the street. You get used to the sound. Felix won the house in a poker game a year before I met him from a guy who operates many of the working oil wells in the area. Berle was built on oil.

When I came through the front door, I spotted my lanky Buddha cross-legged on the built-in hutch blowing a dreamy rendition of Buona Sera on his soprano sax. This was not the first time I'd seen him wedged up there. One must follow one's heart.

He didn't stop playing as I dashed to the kitchen

cupboard for sinus relief. Upon reentering the living room, we held each other's gaze while he finished the tune. I'm sure he was thinking about music, sex or food because that's what he thinks about. I, conversely, was trying to remember where he'd gotten that shirt.

It was a bright orange cotton shirt with two lime green stripes down one side hanging open over a T-shirt. Black and white checked gabardine trousers and one of those straw Bing Crosby hats completed the look. He would have made a great bookie.

"Hey now."

"Hey."

"Baby, you look so pretty."

"Oh, brother." I lifted my specs to rub my eyes.

"Yeah. Like a Sunday supper in Kansas or something."

"That's a very poetic compliment," I said, ambling toward him.

He chuckled, combing his momentarily hatless head with his palm. "You know, like, warm. That's what I'm trying to say."

Felix fingered the keys of his idle horn while he spoke in an attempt to articulate what he was feeling. The saxophone has always been, in his opinion, a better public speaker than he is. I stretched to kiss him but fell short a couple of inches. He unfolded himself and leapt down. I was now looking up at the only part of Felix worth losing.

"Dad, why don't you do something about that goat?"

He automatically stroked his wiry goatee.

"Oh, no. Now you're coming on to me. You better cut that out."

"Honestly, put some conditioner on it. It's starting to look like...like something on a goat."

"You are a bad girl."

He was unbuttoning my beaded sweater-girl sweater. I was letting him.

"Maybe if you let me put a curler in it. Felix, we need to talk."

"About the caper?"

"Yeah."

"Jules, you okay? Your eyes look a little puffy."

"Yeah, I'm fine. I just haven't been sleeping so well."

Somehow, he took that as a green light and continued manipulating the sweater's tiny cloth-covered buttons from their moorings. "You know what might make you sleep better?"

It's true we had a lot of serious talking in front of us that night. It's equally true that I was, at that point, without a sweater.

"You are a temptress! Dance, gypsy, dance!"

This was not the most logical time for lovemaking – for me. Exhausted and hung up on cigars and Cadillacs, I needed to hear myself retell the story digging for clues. Felix, on the other hand, was ready. And when he's ready, he's just so completely ready. Inspiration is such a precious thing.

"Buona sera, signorina. buona sera." he began to croon then suctioned his lips to my shoulder and blew producing the least attractive sound known to woman this side of a fart. "It is time to say good night to Napoli." Snap. Bra on the floor. As he unsnapped it, he threw his arms open and stepped back like 'Tada!' then grabbed my hand and pulled me to him for a moment of semi-nude swing dancing.

"Though it's hard for us to whisper 'buona sera', with that old moon above the Mediterranean Sea. Bazza bazza boop."

"Felix, why don't we ever do this on the bed?"

"Dance?"

"No."

He looked at me as if I'd said "Stick 'em up" then threw me across his shoulder and danced us all the way into the bedroom. I was happy to oblige. After three years I still felt honored every time he touched me.

"By a little jewelry shop we'll stop and linger. Zop. While I buy a wedding ring for your finger. Zoom zoom. In the mean time, let me tell you that I love you. Buona sera, signorina. Kiss me good night."

We decided it was best to take separate cars to the coffeehouse as Felix had that session later on, me in my lovely Saab, him in his chewed-up 1972 Plymouth Fury Grand Coupe. Still, we got there at the same time.

Though we call this place a coffeehouse it's really a club. You can get lunch or dinner. You can get a cocktail. There's a bandstand and dance floor. But there's also a full coffee bar and occasionally people hop up on stage and read poetry so we've always called it the coffeehouse. And I should mention the neon out front says "The Coffeehouse."

We eat here more than we eat at home. Felix sits in with whoever is playing if they ask and he's in the mood. Most of the time there are some very fine session guys hanging out looking to jam while they're off the road. Pretty famous cats, famous in certain circles. The crème de la crème of studio musicians and sidemen.

We sat on the patio. Felix brought his sax to the table for safekeeping.

Rhea took our order and brought our drinks. Felix lit my cigarette and then his own. Nothing left to do now but fill him in.

"Shoot, Luke. You're faded." An expression hulled from a crap game he sauntered into one night. It means hurry up, roll the dice.

"Okay, last night, when you fell asleep on the couch, I tried to write for a while but, you know, nothing, so I went to bed."

He laid his hand over mine and squeezed it. "I'm so glad you told me."

"You're hilarious. There's more."

"Go on."

"Thing is, I didn't stay in bed. Okay, the last couple weeks I've started taking walks at night when you're gone or asleep. I can't seem to sleep right anymore. The walks kind of clear my head."

His bourbon sloshed as he placed it down less-than-gently on the black metal table.

"Jesus, Julie. Like, after 2:00?"

"I can't explain it. It's like I can't stay in bed, like I'm supposed to be someplace only I never know where I'm supposed to be. It's happened every night for the last couple weeks. Weird, huh?"

I waited for him to say something but he just frowned at his drink. "Felix?" I prompted.

"People get mugged and raped when they take walks at two in the morning. That might clear your head. Or you could get yourself murdered. Catch some permanent shut-eye. What a smart fucking wonderful idea, Julie. Jesus! When I'm asleep?"

"Well, I don't think I'll be doing it again so don't freak out."

The food arrived. We began our meal solemnly. Eventually, I found my tongue.

"Look, Felix, this story gets a lot worse."

He rolled his eyes and dropped his fork.

"I think I had some kind of a premonition last night in front of the liquor store."

His expression shifted from icy to frustrated bemusement: the look one gets when an adorable puppy pees where she isn't supposed to.

"You had a premonition."

"Yeah, I think so."

"About what?"

"I'm not sure."

"Come on, Jules." He lifted his glass and examined the bourbon before taking another drink.

"Was that biker there?"

"Sandy. Yeah."

Felix took a deep breath and slowly blew it all out through his mouth. "The fireworks are hailing over little Eden tonight."

"What does that mean? Never mind. Look, I think someone's going to kill him. I think I met her."

I pulled out my fancy new lighter, displayed its true purpose, and placed it between us, then I told him the whole story down to the last detail. By the time the cappuccino arrived he was well informed.

"What should I do? I'd hate to have somebody get hurt and be thinking I could've done something to stop it. I'm thinking there's a lot more going on here than fencing cigars."

Felix had been engrossed and silent throughout.

"So, you kissed the biker?"

"Okay. Totally missing the point."

"I don't think so. I think I can follow it. I'm just looking for a little clarification. You like it?"

I'd never seen him jealous. And though I was uncomfortable with his pedestrian questioning, it was sweet of him to care. I took a moment to internalize how that made me feel and how I should respond. I chose this. "He kissed me."

One furry black eyebrow lifted, his hands bracing the ashtray and bar glass respectively. Then he picked up and pointed the lighter at an imaginary target speaking in a scratchy cowboy purr.

"Maybe I should go kill the son-of-a-bitch my own self." His jaw clenched and eyes narrowed in a mock killer scowl. Then he dropped the bit, crossing his long legs cavalierly. "Whatever, Julie."

I could feel my face blushing. "Are you making fun of me?"

"Nah. Little bit. Forgive me, Jules, but as I think this thing through it occurs to me that you're a very uptight baby. You screwing another guy is just way out. I think you've told me this detail, which you didn't have to, because it's never happened to you before and you're feeling guilty. I mean, baby, you over-analyze every little thing. That's what you do best. So, it's not important. Like, it was a kiss. So, whatever. I don't care."

And with that kind forgiveness he did more than make me feel worthless, he rendered me invisible. He could do that too easily. After all, what was a girl like me...you know. But I couldn't afford to disappear right then. The more ridiculous he made things sound the more profound they became to me. I blinked back the self-doubt about to roll down my face and continued without missing a beat.

"So, what should I do?"

"Absolutely nothing."

I nodded knowing that would be best but dissatisfied with the knowledge.

"Okay. You're right. But look at this." I pushed the lighter toward him. "Why would somebody drop something like that out a window?"

Felix rubbed the barrel with his thumb, looking closely for identifying marks.

"Gee, it's pretty, Jules."

"Pretty unique."

"Maybe she left it as evidence."

"Evidence of what?"

"That she was there."

5

As I pondered that possibility, a guy walked over to the table smiling with his hand extended.

"Hey now!" Felix jumped up and threw his gangly arms around him.

"Julie, baby, this is Charlie Bell. Charles, this is my girlfriend, Julie Page."

I shook his hand while he kissed my cheek.

"Felix the Cat, how have you been, man? You gonna sit in tonight?"

Felix rubbed his chin, considering the question.

"Well, I got a session in a couple hours but maybe. Man, I haven't seen you in months. Where have you been?"

"I don't know, man. I've been around. The house band any good?"

"Yeah, but this isn't the house band. I don't know these people. That guy concerns me." Felix was referring to the man with the perm blowing into the mic as the band set up. "No cats here tonight except you and me, Jackson."

"Mmmm."

"No improvisational pyrotechnics searing the collective consciousness of the whipped-mocha-latte-crunch-with-sprinkles set tonight, Sonny Jim."

"We could change all that, Felix."

"Wake 'em up?"

"Put the fear of God into 'em."

"But, Charlie, they look so peaceful."

"You come over to the table and we'll develop a plan of attack."

"Hip. I got a thing here for a minute so..."

"Sure. Real nice to meet you, Judy."

Felix spoke for me. "It's Julie, you deaf bastard."

The guy made an 'oops' face, smiling as he walked away.

Through all of this inane boy-chatter, I sat mentally scraping the carcass of my liquor store escapade for any last morsel to chew on.

Felix sidled up to me the way he does when he thinks he's been naughty.

"So, where were we?" He tried to put his hand over mine but I needed it to put sugar in my coffee. When I was done, I spoke.

"Isn't that wild that someone would've gone to the trouble to make a fake cigar box? Felix, you smoke a cigar now and then. Ever heard of anything like Montego Supremes?"

"You said it's not a real brand."

"I know. Humor me."

"No, I've never heard of that non-existent cigar. I'm sorry, Judy."

I kicked him. He chuckled.

"Baby, you need to just let this thing slide. I'm not crazy about you getting involved. You don't owe that cocksucker anything. Just leave it alone."

"You really think so?"

"Yes, I really do. Now, I'm gonna go over and catch up with Charley for a minute, okay?"

His eyes started to glaze over as he rose. "Jules, did you say that guy called the old lady Max?"

"Yeah, Max. Why?"

His expression hurled me back to a not-so-happy memory. We were in bed a couple of years ago when I heard the sound of footsteps in the front room. I stuck my elbow into my boyfriend repeatedly, frantically whispering that somebody was in the house. He kept gurgling, "Go back to sleep. There's nobody there." When he finally sat up, presumably to ball me out, we both watched a shadow pass across the hallway. Nobody got hurt and the cops found the guy before he got too far away with the penny-ante stuff he'd stolen but it scared me. Scared Felix, too. A remarkably dark expression washed over his face when he realized there really was an intruder in our house, a look I hadn't seen since. But there it was again. He sat back down.

"My God, Felix, what is it?"

My urgency made him laugh as his typical composure returned.

"Holy cow. Relax, baby. It's nothing. It's just there used to be this singer named Maxine Montego. Just a kooky coincidence. You reminded me of her, that's all."

Here was the morsel I'd been hunting for.

"Who?"

"Maxine Montego. She was a nightclub singer in the '50s, '60s. Real innovator."

"Why haven't I heard of her?"

"Because though I have repeatedly bathed you in

my vast knowingness, you remain a blinded spawn of the great unwashed."

I just stared at him.

"Nobody seems to remember her except musicians. You hear a musician speak of her, it's like, mythic."

"Is she still alive?"

"I don't know. She never calls. Look, Julie, could we talk about this later?" He got back up.

I grabbed his wrist while it was still close enough to grab as clearly we had a lot more to talk about.

"What's she look like, Felix. Anything like the woman I described?"

"Look, there's no possible way. Even if she is alive she'd be into her seventies by now."

"This woman must be about that."

He guffawed. I didn't. "Come on, Jules. Enough. I'm going to go over to Charlie's table now, if that's cool with you. Can we do this later?"

"That's so not cool with me."

He sat back down and looked at the gun. Then he slowly picked it up and held it as if it could help conjure her.

"Okay, let's see. Maxine Montego. She'd stopped working by the time I was old enough to sneak into clubs but I heard the story more than once over the years. In fact, my sax teacher, Mr. Randolph, gave me a couple of her records before he retired. I'd say Maxine Montego helped make me a much cooler twelve-year-old than I would've otherwise been. Hey, you saw those records, remember? When we were boxing up all that stuff for storage when you moved in. You thought she was pretty."

"I almost remember that. So, she was famous?"

He shrugged. "No mass popularity to speak of. She was too edgy for the mainstream back then. Her lyrics were a little out there. Like, dense. She fit more into a measure than your average bear. Unconventional, I guess you'd say." He put the gun back between us and smiled at me.

"So it was this unconventional writing that made her mythic?"

"No. Well, yes, it was that and this thing that happened."

He licked the concave part of his spoon then tried to suspend it from his prominent nose. I remained unimpressed as the spoon crashed to the table.

"Are you going to make me ask you what the thing was or are you just going to tell me?"

"I'm trying to remember how it came down."

He leaned back in the chair, drumming his elegant fingers over the horn case.

"The way the story goes is, like, everything was going great. Maxine was Queen of the Sunset Strip. Eventually she gets bored with that and decides to take on Vegas. This is in the mid-50s, I think. So, she gets a gig at the Sahara and she's building a serious following, when all of a sudden she gets sick. Real sick. Pneumonia or something. Guess who they get to fill her dates."

"Don't make me guess."

"Louis Prima."

"You were just playing Buona Sera."

"Louis fucking Prima. His popularity went like, zoom. Overnight he's the talk of the town and Maxine Montego is out on her ear."

"And you were just playing that song!"

"Why do you keep saying that? I like the song."

"I don't know. Go on."

"So, she leaves Vegas, devastated about losing this spot. I don't know why that one thing was supposed to have done her in. Maybe just one too many sucker punches like that. Who knows? But legend has it that's maybe when she started to go a little cuckoo."

Felix had to talk louder as the band banged through a ridiculous medley that was currently working over "Rocket Man." The singer was doubled over with emotion (or something) as sweat dripped off of his store-bought tan. Charlie Bell took his fingers out of his ears long enough to wave goodbye on his way out the door. Felix waved back.

"She starts drinking."

"What?"

"Drinking. She starts playing less-than-fabulous joints. Reno. Riverside. Anything. I guess she didn't want to go back to the Strip."

"Speak up. I can barely hear you."

"Sorry. She probably didn't care where she was playing. I mean, at least she was working. This is when they say she really got into her songwriting. Cut a few 45s, a few albums."

"So, once she knew fame had passed her by she could afford to get creative."

"You're very deep."

We were now yelling over the wounded animal on stage. I gestured for Felix to go on.

"Then, at this club in Jersey, I think it was '67, '68, a fire broke out in the kitchen, which was supposedly closed by show time. By the time anyone knew there was a fire it was way out of control."

I watched a vein protrude from Felix's forehead

as he valiantly competed with the din in the room. The bartender turned the jukebox on to drown out the "entertainment" but, apparently, the band could not take a hint. Every toupee on stage continued wagging back and forth. I shot my head toward the singer with a very angry look and inadvertently caught his eye. He winked and extended his index finger at me as if I'd requested a song and not his resignation. It was absurd. I half expected to see a midget walk through the club balancing a balloon on his head.

"Okay, so, I guess people were running and falling and screaming and all the things you do when you're stuck in a fire. They say Maxine kept singing when the band started to bail. They say when she finally did figure out that the show wasn't going on she just stands there like that crazy gal in... What's that movie with the crazy gal?"

"Streetcar Named Desire."

"What? No. The one with what's her name."

"Barton Fink."

"Come on!"

"Sunset Boulevard."

"Yeah."

"There's no fire in Sunset Boulevard."

"Whatever. She stands there, flames all around her, and waits. Nobody knows what she was thinking. I mean, did she think those people were going to take care of her first or was she saying, like, I'm working, I'm staying here? They say no one even tried to get her out of the club, no one until an ambulance came."

As Felix persevered, the knuckleheads on stage finally jumped off so we could all take a break. There was no applause. Now, with only the civilized hum of the crowd and jukebox to contend with, I unclenched my fists and Felix leaned back.

"Jeez. That guy was making me hate my own kind. Where was I? Oh, so, there were different reports about her at the time. The common take was that she died in the hospital. Another story was that she eventually healed and moved back to LA where she made a living recording books for the blind. The incident didn't make as many headlines as you'd think, like it was hushed up or something. Maxine Montego just disappeared."

"It's her."

"Jules, no, baby. That can't be right."

"You're the one who brought her up. If I didn't know better, I'd say you were having your own premonition."

This is where Felix might have explained what a ridiculous idea that was, but he didn't. Instead, he pensively trawled the air with his eyes, ruminating. I knew he was trying to figure what the odds were on a thing like that.

"I don't know, Julie, maybe it was her. How weird would that be?"

He took out his cigarette pack and tapped it several times against his other hand, tamping down the tobacco like he does before lighting up. Then he shoved them back in his pocket.

"Okay, wait. This is insane. Maxine Montego would not drive around in the middle of the night so as to wrap duct tape around some liquor store clerk and steal his cigars. It wasn't Maxine Montego."

"It was somebody."

"I'm going to go on over to that Costello session now." He was squeezing my shoulder. "I'll bet he remembers Maxine Montego. He's like some kind of musical encyclopedia. It's kind of creepy, the amount of shit he knows. Listen, don't go looking for any inspiration tonight. Hear me?"

"Elvis Costello?"

He squatted to look me in the eye.

"No, Lou Costello. Don't have anymore adventures, Jules, okay? I need you to be all right. Just go to bed. Please."

"Why don't I get to hang out with Elvis Costello?"

"He says he doesn't like you."

"Good night, Felix."

The band made its way back to the bandstand with the singer sporting a costume change incorporating a blue sequined shirt with a stand-up collar.

"Oh, no. No-no." Felix kissed my hand and stood up fast. "If I don't leave right now, I swear to God, an artery is going to burst out the side of my neck. Be good."

He flew out the door just as the band launched into "Song Sung Blue."

I can't explain exactly how I knew the woman who ran into Bob's Liquor Palace was, indeed, Maxine Montego. Maybe I had seen those albums of Felix's. At least that would explain why she looked familiar. Besides, if it was Maxine, I already knew something about her. If it wasn't, I had nothing.

Someone toward the front of the club threw an olive at the singer. It bounced off his forehead and he didn't even blink. When he went to twirl his mic around by the cable, it flew off, leaving him mute. The crowd cheered.

6
◇◇◇◇◇◇◇

My thoughts were all about Maxine on the ride home. She made for a fascinating story without any additional cigar stealing intrigue. I wondered what this mythic music of hers had sounded like, what she had sounded like before she lost that Vegas gig. And I wondered at the actual distance between that girl and the woman she had become. How much of yourself can you burn and still be alive?

The house was dark and I didn't bother to turn on a light. I stood for a moment staring into the blackness, finally focusing on my lonely Hermes 3000 typewriter waiting patiently on the corner desk. "Not tonight," I thought, "I'm not even gonna try tonight."

Opening the back door, I leaned against the frame and lit a cigarette. If it was Maxine Montego, why in the world would she have her name on a box of cigars?

I flipped on the Malibu lights. As I stood thinking how nicely manicured our little yard was, it occurred to me that Felix and I never really spent any time out there. That's why the backyard looked so good. A mural of the Louvre covered the cinder block fence. Colorful renderings of famous works of art encircled the tiki torches and plastic flamingos dotting the grass. The mural had been a gift from a painter friend of mine, a friend I hadn't seen since shortly after moving in. It was good-natured of Felix to let him paint his fence, I thought. But those friends were long gone now. My life had gotten very small since moving into the Craftsman on Poppy, only big enough to house my sobriety and Felix.

I stood at the kitchen door staring at that fence. It made me think of Sandy. He, too, was a colorful fence. I couldn't fight it. I had to check on him. One more late night walk for posterity. Felix would never have to know.

My impatient strides carried me pretty far for the first ten minutes or so but when I hit the east side of Vanguard, I felt myself slow down. I passed Meads Drug, Wanda's House of Hair, but this time each shop stuck its foot out as I walked by as if the buildings were trying to tell me something, something like only an idiot would go back to that liquor store after last night. The buildings were making sense.

Seriously dragging my feet by the time I hit The Cat's Meow, I decided to wait for a moment under the green neon glow of a cat lifting his top hat and then putting it back on in perpetual motion. I counted the dead flies lining the window sill illuminated by a Budweiser sign.

"Just another tired neighborhood in a dirty little town called Home. Damn, that's good. I gotta write that down. Well, hello, Doris."

It was Carroll slowly waving an unlit cigarette up and down in front of his mouth, unintentionally mimicking the neon cat's movements.

"How'd you know where to find me?"

"Hi, Carroll." I pulled out my very special lighter. He tried to jump back in shock but it just looked like he was doing a bad Bette Davis impression. I lit his smoke.

"Isn't that the cutest thing you have ever seen! Oh, Bertha! That's a gem. You got me. You got me good. Hey, you're a writer. I got something I want to show you. This baby's going to make me a wealthy man. It's a little something I like to call 'Sad Teeth.' Where are my goddamn keys? Oh."

He opened the unlocked door of a Honda Civic parked right outside the bar. The keys were hanging from the ignition, probably because it would prove to be too difficult getting them back in there once the cocktails went to work. His skinny butt kept me company while he fished around in the backseat. When he came up for air, he was empty handed.

"It's actually a compost of poetry and prose I've collected over the years. I must've left it back at the motel. I call it 'Sad Teeth.' How would you like to read that, missy?" He staggered back by the padded, studded door and tried to land the cigarette in his mouth.

"Maybe some other time, Carroll."

I was almost happy to see him. It was keeping me from facing what was around the corner. But, all too soon, we had company.

"Hey." This vision appeared in the doorway. "You trying to make me jealous, Carroll?" This vision of running mascara and brittle, ratted hair.

Her stretch pants were doing just that and her cowgirl shirt seemed to have been designed by the same guy who put together the front door, silver studs and all. It would be pure supposition on my part to say that she'd been around, but she looked like she'd been poked more times than the Pillsbury Dough Boy.

Carroll turned from me and saddled up to his obvious weakness – someone who wanted to talk to him. He went to put his hand on her, no doubt trying to focus on where she was. In an attempt to make contact, his hand found her sit-upon.

She began to laugh then went into a coughing jag that lasted long enough to both embarrass and concern me. Slithering back inside, she baited him to try for more and he followed, post haste. Our conversation was over.

I started to walk on when I saw a figure standing in the shadows of Munson's Used Car Lot across the street. It was him, Maxine's friend. He was standing with his feet apart, hands clasped in front of him and looking right at me.

Though he was literally in the shadows and though I couldn't see his face from under his hat, I had no doubt it was him. The car he stood in front of was not Munson's usual fare.

The Cadillac looked beautiful and imposing half lit by the year-round Christmas bulbs behind it. Strings of red plastic flags crisscrossed Munson's lot snapping in the strong breeze. Sounded like wings. All these elements collected, it felt like a dream; like I was looking at an enchanted hearse with a benevolent Death waiting patiently at the door for me to climb inside.

Walking over to him seemed like a scary thing to do and running away seemed childish and unwarranted. I chose to stand very still. He touched the brim of his hat and nodded once. I nodded back. Then he got in that big black car and pulled out of Munson's onto 5th Street, heading west.

Only then did I realize that I was standing too close to the street and too far away from the neon cat to be visible. He couldn't see me. No, he was looking at someone else, someone I couldn't see from where I was, someone in front of Bob's Liquor Palace. And he had just given a signal.

Like seeing a dog run into traffic, I couldn't get to Sandy in time to save him now, assuming he was even there.

My impulses were conflicted as I watched Maxine's friend pull out of sight. I wanted to know what was about to happen at the liquor store, I wanted to get out of there fast, and I really wanted to know where that Cadillac was going.

Then, I did the single oddest thing I've ever done in my entire life. Without much hesitation at all, I got in Carroll's Honda and took off down 5th Street, heading west.

7

I didn't even glance at the liquor store as I passed, racing down the dark, empty street. He must've been pretty darn preoccupied. I can't think of another reason why he didn't notice me. Having never chased anyone before, I had no skill at it and there weren't any other cars to hide behind.

I followed him into the hills. The streets narrowed. Streetlights were fewer and farther between. No longer in the urban grit of the city, I was now looking down upon it. Deceptively lovely from that angle. And the neighborhood I suddenly found myself in was lovely any way you look at it.

Each of these houses has an insulating stretch of yard between it and the next. Lawn jockeys and Saint Francis statuary freckle various walkways standing sentinel, inviting you up but checking your invitation at the door.

When he stopped, he stopped abruptly at the curb barely taking time to close the car door. He hustled up the drive and after some brief lock fiddling, entered the house. It was a sprawling, ranch style model, one story, two chimneys, three-car garage.

Parking one yard away in an attempt to maintain

anonymity, I found myself walking sideways along the periphery of the roses and hyacinth lining the drive. I stopped next to a large picture window where a lot of yelling was going on. Light shone through partially closed wooden shutters just enough to let me know I'd found the action.

The yelling stopped as I approached. Then there was a loud crash of glass shattering. When the conversation resumed, voices were low and words measured.

"I'm telling you, my hands are clean. Happy Man just wanted confirmation. He didn't want any unnecessary accidents." His voice sounded like gravel.

"Unnecessary accidents? Peter, have you lost your mind?" Hers was the voice of authority.

No one said anything for several seconds, then...

"What should I have done? What the hell was I supposed to do?"

Though I couldn't literally see them, in my mind I could. Like getting lost in the characters of some great radio theatre, I leaned my head against the wall listening intently, imagining.

"A line's been crossed, Peter. No one was supposed to get hurt. And if I find out Sandy has been hurt..."

"I told you..."

"Yes, I know what you told me. If I find out he's been hurt, the rules change. I picked him. I chose him arbitrarily, poor slob."

"He knew the box always came to you, Max. He knew he shouldn't give it to anybody else."

"Jesus Christ, Peter, he didn't even have a way to call me. A delivery van dropped it off and I picked it up. That was it. He certainly didn't grasp the grandeur of the operation. That was his charm. That's what made him perfect."

After another moment of silence, Peter tried again to defend his actions.

"Happy Man would not have liked it if that box had disappeared. Hell, I probably saved your life tonight."

She laughed sardonically. "Peter, you kill me."

The clink of leaded crystal told me a drink was being poured.

"You know, the Thai boys were never thrilled about using your name on those boxes, Maxine."

I felt like a gal who'd just spent her last buck on a lottery ticket and got all six numbers. This was Maxine Montego. I was right. Felix was wrong.

"Ballsy. Completely unnecessary."

"Everybody's a critic."

It seemed by his tone that he was gently trying to redirect the finger pointing straight at him. But if Maxine's tone was any indication, that wasn't going to work.

"Look, now that I'm sitting and medicated, explain to me what happened slowly and precisely."

"What was I supposed to do?"

"Here, I'll start," she interjected. "The reason I was called to pick up the box early was because those delivery kids had other plans for it, I suppose."

"Right. Only one of the two delivery guys ever met the clerk. The other guy always stayed in the van. There was only one guy he could recognize."

"Wake me when you start to explain what happened."

"Their plan was to drop off a box of Montego Supremes as usual but this time, tell the clerk that somebody else would pick it up. Told him you'd be back the following week. Paid him for the inconvenience."

"Well, I've got the box. We let Sandy know we were disappointed. And I'll hold it, as asked, until things cool down. Why the drama?"

"Max, you know better than that. And besides, they were going to frame the clerk."

"I'm listening."

"The other guy was supposed to show up two days later wearing a disguise, pick up the box, then split the profits with the other one."

"Why would he wear a disguise if Sandy had never seen him before?"

"Because when the box came up missing, somebody was gonna go down for it, either you or the clerk or the delivery drivers who actually did it. So, if the guy picking up the box had a believable disguise, the clerk wouldn't be able to finger him. Odds are Happy Man wouldn't suspect you and that leaves the clerk. One of the Thai boys would take him out quickly and quietly and they'd get away with it, nice and clean."

"You use that word too often lately."

"What word?"

"Clean."

"Give it a rest, Max. Please."

I heard the flint of a lighter being used then tossed indelicately onto some hard surface. He continued.

"Apparently, the van was wired. One of them slipped and said too much. Thailand knew everything. That's when they told you to pick up the box a day early."

"I see." She sounded tired.

"So, when the dumb shits showed up tonight to cop the box, one of 'em in a red suit, no less, somebody other than the clerk was behind the counter waiting for him and somebody else was out front. They just wanted me to confirm these were the right delivery guys. That's all." His voice trailed off.

"That's all." Maxine repeated, quietly.

"There won't be any more deliveries, okay? We've seen the last box of Montego Supremes. They're going to get rid of the van tonight. Look, that guy didn't know enough for Happy Man to want him dead."

"Peter, you don't know that. You don't have a clue."

He harrumphed. "Well, it doesn't matter because he wasn't there when the mob showed up."

Then I kicked the wall. My knee locked, and when I drew back my foot to unlock it, I smacked the wall with the heel of my Delaney boot. Clever girl.

"What the hell was that?" Peter said.

Even running as fast as I could, the car seemed miles from where I was. Once safely inside, I looked back at the house.

Peter came flying out the front door. Maxine stood at the window, her arms extended and head angled to see between the slats of the shutters. Made me think of a crucifixion.

As I tried to unwind down the hill, I stayed glued to the rear view mirror. Nothing. How lucky could I be? When familiar landmarks came into view, I relaxed a little.

I couldn't believe what I'd heard. I couldn't believe I'd been so right about the gravity of the situation. Mostly and above all else, I couldn't believe I was driving a stolen car.

I wanted to feel worse about it than I did, but, you know, it worked. It paid off. The ethics sacrificed seemed insignificant compared to what I'd gained. Still, I'd stolen a car. That wasn't right. I had to get it back to the bar as quickly and safely as possible, ready to face the consequences.

But nothing could've prepared me for what I saw as I approached the now-too-popular corner of 5th and Vanguard. Yellow tape and orange cones veered people around and away from Bob's Liquor Palace. There were cops and ambulance drivers everywhere, inside and out.

A sweet new Thunderbird convertible with one wheel on the curb and a headlight hugging a parking meter looked like something out of a Stephen King book. The shiny white interior was covered with blood, more blood than I'd ever seen, thick and dark. I winced and closed my eyes but when I opened them I was still staring at someone's guts.

Rolling forward a couple more feet, I tried to see inside the liquor store but couldn't see much, just plenty of police and a splattering of red running down the glass door I'd used on so many occasions. Red Suit must've been shot inside and his partner, in the T-bird. Sandy's adventure was making me sick to my stomach.

Nausea and tears were put on hold as a policewoman approached the car. I thought about blurting out everything I knew but something kept me from it.

"You have business here, miss?"

I leaned into the car so she could do the same.

"No, just... What happened?"

"Police business. I'm going to have to ask you to

clear the area. Thanks." She started to back away. Then among a small crowd of bar patrons across the street, Carroll saw his car.

"Hey! What the hell are you doing? That's my car!"

The policewoman turned back around. Speeding away at that point would not have served me well, so I waited until he stumbled over.

"Is this the car, sir? Can I see license and registration, miss? This gentleman lost a car earlier this evening."

"What the hell are you doing in my car, Doris?"

She pulled back the flashlight that had been lighting the inside of the car and turned it on Carroll.

"You know this woman, sir?"

"Well, of course he does. Come on, Carroll. Get in. The officer wants us out of the area while they're working. He gets confused sometimes. I don't let him drive when he's in this condition."

I was lying like I sold lies for a living.

"What the HELL is going on here?" His eyes were as big as cocktail coasters. The policewoman readjusted her watch as she glanced at it.

"Okay, let's move. I'm glad you found your car, sir. Now, please clear the area."

"What are you talking about, lady? Get out of my car, Doris!"

"Sir, I need for you to let her drive you home. Let's go. We've got work to do."

"But she stole my mother loving car!"

I smiled knowingly at her and sputtered an embarrassed, "I'm sorry."

"Get in the car, sir."

"Carroll, let's go. They're busy. Let's get some

coffee and you tell me about that book." I opened the passenger door from the inside.

"Well, that's just the craziest! Why are you in my car?"

He was ranting but he got in. The cop waved us on as another officer approached her. I didn't like the pressure of being a car thief.

"Christ, Cherry's is right around the corner if you want some goddamn coffee," he snapped, as the car door closed.

8

◇◇◇◇◇◇

Cherry's is a 24-hour coffee shop a couple blocks up town. Carroll was expecting me to buy him a cup of coffee and chat with him about his book, so I did.

I don't know. I needed the cops to see us drive off together. I wanted to calm him down and get him out of there before he went yapping about anything incriminating, like meeting me the night before where all the blood was.

He ordered chili and I ordered coffee. He talked about his poetry and I thought about dead bodies. He shared his views on everyone from James Joyce to Joyce Brothers and I tried to imagine where Sandy could possibly run and not get caught, if he was lucky enough to still be alive. But when Carroll started to talk about the horror that had just taken place at the neighborhood liquor store, I started to cry, real loud.

"Hey, what's wrong with you?"

"I'm sorry, man. I...I..."

"Oh for Pete's sake, Doris. Pull yourself together."

Something about him saying this made me laugh, which bothered him further.

"Get a grip on yourself. They can refuse service, you know." For the first time since I met him, he spoke in hushed tones.

"I've got to go. Thanks for the..."

"Car?"

I needed to tidy that up. "No, I was going to say conversation. Look, you asked me to drive your car, Carroll." I placed the keys on the table.

"I did?"

He was no longer sure and that's all I needed him to be.

"Here, let me get this." I put a ten on the table and buttoned my coat on the way to the door.

"I'm not sure I can see you anymore, Doris. Don't call me until you straighten up." He was now speaking in his usual amplified manner adding as I waved goodbye, "Straighten up and fly right, Doris, or LOSE MY NUMBER."

As soon as I got safely home, I dropped my clothes and dove into bed just as if I thought I might sleep. There was no possibility of me actually sleeping but Felix didn't know that. He got home about an hour after me, thank God, and tried to be quiet as he readied himself for bed. His silent presence provided some comfort.

I laid there with my eyes closed, more alert than I'd ever been. Surely the phone would ring and it would be the cops. Surely I was guilty of something. I could still go to the authorities, but once again, I didn't know who would ultimately get hurt if I did. Somebody needed to protect Maxine.

I felt an illogical tie to the old woman and wanted to believe her worthy of my protective instincts. I wanted to believe her anger was somehow justified, an unwitting participant, guilty by association but innocent of anything more substantive. Besides, she had such style.

Work the next day was the biggest drag ever. Who gave a shit about Monday Night football flyers and banners for the Health and Fitness Expo?

This time I didn't show up to hit a deadline, I showed up so as to not let on that anything out of the ordinary had taken place the night before. And frankly, I was afraid to break my pattern. Were I to in any way deviate from my regular routine, everything good and safe I'd woven into my tattered life might come unraveled. One good pull on one loose thread, that's all it would take, and I knew it. Work would save me for one more day. I could think things out there. I could sleep.

Of course, it is a local newspaper we're talking about and the murders were being discussed at every water cooler. I avoided all conversations that revolved around the harsh crime and pretended, however unconvincingly, to keep my nose to the grindstone. My boss met me as I got off the elevator and he was getting on.

"Morning, Julie. Say, where are we with the automotive promo? Oh, and have we wrapped up the insertions for the circus ads?"

I didn't know what the hell he was talking about.

"Yes," I said.

"Good job."

The workday expired without incident. I turned the radio up on the drive home in an attempt to drown out the pounding in my head, but even on the jazz station, double homicide was the top story of the day.

"Two Asian men in their mid-twenties were found

murdered last night at the corner of 5th and Vanguard sometime around midnight. Each man shot through the head and chest, execution style, in one of the most curious double homicides in recent memory."

The reporter went on to say that one of these guys, the one in the red suit, was wearing a wig as well as a prosthetic nose. The other was out front in what was being considered the get-away car. From former convictions, the cops had traced the two to an international crime ring headquartered in Thailand.

Between the bizarre disguise, the fact that nothing was taken, and the disappearance of the clerk who should've been tending the counter, the media was having a field day. Sandy was being considered a suspect.

They said the murders were connected to an elusive mob boss known only as Happy Man who ran an import/export business from Thailand. The gentleman had never been convicted and hardly ever seen, but was widely regarded as one of the world's preeminent diamond smugglers. The media had dubbed the dark scene at the Liquor Palace "The Happy Man Murders."

So, it was diamonds. How very Raymond Chandler of her. Maxine had been told to go pick up a box of diamonds a couple of days earlier than usual. That created a whole other list of questions, the most pressing of which was why her?

Home was not where my heart was. I came through the front door aching from exhaustion and nerves. Felix had left a note by the phone. Apparently, they had asked him to put together a band for the coffeehouse that night as the other band had been dismissed.

He and the crew he'd drummed up were at the coffeehouse for a quick once over with charts and such. At the bottom of the note, he added, "PS - Baby, I found this today at that used record store I was telling you about. Asked on a lark if they carried any of her stuff. You're a lucky girl. I'll try to find those albums in the storage unit later."

He had put the 45 on the turntable for me. I gently placed the needle on the vinyl. The A side was a swing number called "Closer to the Hip."

I'm down for the count,
The referee has said good night
How can you win
When you are paid to throw the fight?
Turning in my pointless punches
For a round of business lunches
And now I want to be a member of the bourgeoisie
Happy just to be lost in anonymity – bop
I'm no better than you, honey
Okay, I might be, maybe
I'm not gonna push nobody
Closer to, closer to the hip
And when I finally figured out better is never bigger
Now, the safety is on my trigger
Closer to, closer to the hip

I carefully turned the disc over. The flip side was a song called "Saturday Night."

She wasn't as pretty as the girls he could see
He wasn't as charming as he thought he was –
Who could be?
But the club was deserted
So they both got in for free

At the bar – she gave up the ghost
He gave up the quest
She reached for a cigarette, he reached for his vest
And offered her a light, Saturday night
The sign on the motel made some dangerous claims
They slunk to their bungalow
Exchanging their adopted names
The room was a mirror ball
Reflecting countless shames
Once inside – she gave up the ghost
He gave up the quest
She reached for a buckle and he reached for a dress
Someone hit the light, Saturday night

Yes, these words would seem perfectly natural coming out of the droll, articulate woman I'd spied on the night before. And as much as I'd learned about this retired chanteuse in the last three days, I knew shit until I heard her music. She was truly something. How could people have forgotten her?

I played the disc over and over, each time growing more attached to the artist. She sounded utterly invincible. It moved me to hear her so young, before Louis Prima and burn wards and diamond smugglers had adjusted her priorities. Where does inspiration go when it leaves? When had it deserted her?

A strong wave of empathy crashed over me. Tears fell effortlessly without wrinkling my brow. This isn't how things were supposed to turn out is a sentiment shared by the bulk of humanity, I suppose.

I got to thinking about that book I wrote four years ago and about what I'd lost along the way: jobs, savings, friendships, health. But I'll bet Maxine would concur that when you wake up every morning feeling brilliant, nothing else matters much, not at the time.

That book didn't get published. Come to find out, no one was interested. I thought about writing another book but decided instead to make a series of bad choices and wallow in self-pity until inspiration came rushing back, begging forgiveness.

Thing is, you might convince inspiration to stay for a couple of hours but you can't always get it to spend the night. Inspiration can run to the corner for a pack of smokes and never comes back at all. And most of the time that which we call inspiration is just a dry, academic process: a brutal, unromantic exercise in patience. Some of us weather it, some of us don't.

9

✧✧✧✧✧✧

The 45 spun idle now. The sound of the needle hitting the label brought my attention back to the moment at hand. Gently removing the vinyl, I slid it into its insufficient paper sleeve and tucked it between the speaker and bobble-head Shriner for safekeeping.

Yes, Maxine Montego had a new fan and I deeply wished things were coming down differently for her, but they weren't. I had to tell Felix what had transpired overnight. It was too much information to process alone. Maybe he would know what to do. I didn't.

I arrived at the coffeehouse in five minutes instead of my usual ten. The band was finishing up a number as I made my way to the bar. They sounded great.

When the song ended, musicians were milling around the stage going over whatever chart was the next point of interest, everyone but the fellow I'd met two nights ago, Charlie Bell. He continued playing the piano, barreling through random snippets of songs, one after the other.

I ordered a cup of coffee. Before it hit the cup, the room exploded in a burst of hometown pride. I turned in time to see Charlotte Vaughn take her place at the mic. I guess she weaseled out of the last set of her own gig when Felix called, trouper that she is.

Felix took the mic for a brief introduction.

"We're gonna do one more number before we take a little break and I think this nice lady is gonna help us out. Do you need me to tell you who this is?" Everybody cheered. "Charlotte Vaughn. Give it up." People were hooting and clapping until she gestured for them to sit down.

"Felix called me tonight and said he was in a fix. So he reached into his bag of tricks and guess what, I was one of the tricks."

I found a place to lean at the bar as the boys kicked things off with a riff that had the crowd tapping their feet and snapping their fingers almost immediately. Then, out of nowhere, the horn section blasted a hole in the back wall with this atonal, harmonically challenged gale, creating a thrilling kind of chaos.

When the drummer couldn't contain himself any longer, he stood up, threw his head back, and hollered like a banshee as he beat the shit out of the floor toms. We felt his joy.

Char stepped up front and center, spread her legs, and put her hands on her ample hips. She wore a red peek-a-boo blouse and sequined bell-bottom pants, which dangled just above her spiky Louboutins. The cappuccino machine fell silent out of respect.

Engaging a strong sense of irony, she waxed eloquently through a lengthy arrangement of Beck Hansen's "Where It's At" with the band capably supporting her every cue. Whenever she shot her arm out to the side, the boys behind her complied with a resounding, "Where it's at." Then, Char. "I got two turn-tables and a microphone." It was all so much fun I almost forgot what I was there for. Almost.

"Charlotte Vaughn," Felix shouted. The audience did clap their hands as the talent took five. I made my way to the stage in time to say hi to her while waiting for Felix to stop beating his chest and come over.

"You are really something, toots. That was hot."

She squatted down to chat. "Hi, sugar. Damn, twice in one week. Kind of like old times. You doing any better than the other day?"

"Not really, Char, no."

A young buck saddled up to the stage next to me with a hand extended and love in his eyes. "Excuse me, Ms. Vaughn. My name's Antoine and I'm surely you're biggest fan. I wonder, while you're on a break, if I might buy you a cocktail. It would be such an honor."

Charlotte took his hand and turned to me. "Julie, call me tomorrow, okay? I think Antoine and I have plans." She stood up and started for the steps then looked back my way. "Call me tomorrow?"

I shook my head up and down wondering what tomorrow would even look like then turned my attention to Felix who was chatting with Charlie Bell.

"No, man. I think Beck would get a kick out of that."

Mr. Bell replied, "I'm not a hundred percent on that, Felix, but I've definitely got an erection."

Felix eventually knelt down so we could talk.

"Hey now. Did you get my present?"

"You've never given me a finer gift. Maxine Montego was definitely amazing."

"Mythic. Let me come down there. Got a table?"

"No, I just got here. That was some performance."

"Are you coming on to me?"

He put one hand around my neck and the other around a drink heading toward the patio. There was one table available against the back fence. As we settled in and lit up, a couple came bounding over. The young man spoke.

"You are fucking awesome, dude."

His date had this overly cartoonish look of amazement on her mug.

"Thank you, my brother." Felix was both relaxed and energized like he gets when he plays.

I tried to keep a pleasant look on my face as I spoke. "So, have you heard the news today?"

His expression remained happy but his forehead showed concern. Then his expression did change, unfavorably.

"No, Julie. I haven't. But if it involves another late night adventure, you can spare me the details, all right?"

"What's that supposed to mean?"

"I mean, if you've done something stupid or dangerous, I don't want to hear it."

"It's not like that."

"When did this Honey West complex set in anyway?"

"Who?"

"Get me. My girlfriend is Emma fucking Peel."

He looked so disgusted. This was going to be harder than I thought.

"Calm down. Christ. Why assume that I'm going to tell you anything about me at all? Give me a break."

It took a beat or two but eventually he released the muscles in his face.

"Jeez, I'm sorry, baby. I just... This whole Maxine thing has me a little freaked out. Something does. Gives me the creeps. Why is that?" He took my hand. "Jules, I'm truly sorry. Here, give me some tongue."

I pushed him away, both of us grinning apologetically.

"So, what were you going to report before you were so rudely interrupted?"

How could I tell him what happened after that?

Right then, Jack the waiter came over retying his apron in a hurry so he could shake Felix's hand, his admiration obvious. He said the owner wanted to know if we wanted anything from the kitchen. Tonight, it was on the house.

"I don't know, man. I've got to go back up there in a minute. Jules?"

Before I could answer, Jack decided to ruin my evening.

"Hey, Julie, did you hear about those guys getting shot at the Liquor Palace last night? Oh, man! Un-believable. Unbefuckinglievable."

I no longer had to find a right way to break the news.

"Yeah, Jack. Unbelievable. You know, I'm not hungry. Thanks anyway."

The waiter walked away nodding his head one way, indicating that he understood me, and then the other way, indicating that he still couldn't believe what had happened at the neighborhood liquor store. I followed him with my eyes as long as I could, not wanting to look across the table.

"You and I have nothing to say to each other right now." With that, Felix got up and started to leave.

"Look, hey, I understand that you're pissed, Felix, all right? But I'm real scared and I'm probably in real trouble. So, why don't we skip the how-dare-you bullshit, okay?"

He stared at me long after I shut up, eventually looking less angry and more scared himself.

"We'll talk about it tonight. I've gotta go to work."

He took a couple of steps, paused, and turned around. "I've got one more set. I'll be home in about two hours."

He cued his band mates as he walked by them one at a time, and one at a time, each rose to join him. He put out his hand for Charlotte when approaching her table and they walked hand-in-hand to the stage. As they presented themselves again as a unit, before playing a note, the crowd gave a unanimous standing ovation. Felix Mint. Amen.

The drive home was lonely. That's the most accurate way to describe it. I'd never been so estranged from Felix. He'd never pulled away like that before.

As soon as I got home I took a much-needed shower and wrapped myself in that big robe of mine, curled up on the couch, and watched the front door. As promised, Felix walked through it a little after 2:00. He put down his horn case then gently sat on the coffee table in front of me. Our knees were touching. "Okay. How bad is it?"

I started to answer but got all choked up. He dropped his chin to his chest and waited while I regrouped. Pulling it together enough to tell him about stealing the car and the spying, I explained the whole

'Happy Man' thing as I understood it. But in describing the blood and glass and yellow tape, I fell apart again, crying and shaking uncontrollably as each dirty detail landed on his sensitive ears.

Felix put his hand on my leg in an attempt to steady me. I just got louder. He carefully climbed onto the couch and laid on top of me until I stopped.

When it was merely a matter of catching my breath, he sat up. Then I sat up.

"This is where I say, 'Thanks, I needed that,' right?"

"How 'bout you don't say anything for a minute. I'm going to talk." He was awfully upset.

"You know that premonition you had in front of the liquor store? Well, my sixth sense has been pretty active lately, too. Every time I look at you lately, I almost don't see you anymore. Like, we used to be connected and now, I don't know. I just want to be able to see you without looking twice."

"I'm still here. I just can't ignore what's going on right now. That's all. I don't want to ignore it."

"You need to call the cops. You're going to get into all kinds of trouble if you keep crawling around in other people's shit. Even if the shit belongs to..." he smiled incredulously at the ceiling then resumed our discussion. "...Maxine Montego, whatever that's about."

"She might get hurt if I call the cops now."

"Who cares? I need you to pull your head out of your butt. You've made it painfully clear I can't do it for you."

"If I were smarter, I'd figure out a way to undo this thing that's about to happen. Believe me, I know

I sound like an idiot but I think she needs me, or something. I think I'm supposed to help her."

He slapped his hands over his cheeks. "Jesus Christ!"

"Well, something. I don't think I fell into this for no reason. There's got to be a reason. It's too outrageous."

"Here's what would be outrageous. You getting killed because your craning neck was stuck in the wrong place at the wrong time. And I've got a flash for you, smart-ass. I need you."

His voice broke when he said that, his voice and my heart.

"What do you want me to do?"

"Call the fucking cops. I just said that." He uncharacteristically banged the kitchen chair against the linoleum tile.

"I can't. Okay? I can't do that. I was there that night. I was there the night before. I knew something awful was going to happen, remember? The cops might not be all that friendly right now. A cop even talked to me that night. I lied to her face. I need some time. I need to just follow whatever it is that's pulling at me, try to stay calm and trust my instincts."

He let out an ironic cackle.

"Oh, yeah, baby. Your instincts have served you so well. One missing person and two dead men later, you're going to save the day, you and a one hundred year-old, charbroiled lounge singer. You go, girl."

"Shut up, Felix. Just shut the fuck up!"

He kicked the La-Z-Boy recliner with his foot hard enough to move it, walked over by the turntable, and picked up the 45. He pulled it from its sleeve and waved it in my face. I had never seen this side of my better half.

"Felix, put it down."

"This bitch is ruining our lives."

He grabbed the disc by both sides and shoved it toward me like a tiny hors d'oeuvre tray. Boy, did I want him to put that record down.

"Only hours ago she was mythic."

"Well, she's not now. She's way real. Too real. She's the real end."

"Okay, just snap it in half. I mean, if it would make you feel better. Would you feel better if you snapped it in half, Felix? It's only music. It's just a fragile little recording. Who cares about shit like that?"

He threw his head back and collapsed his shoulders, dropping his arms to his sides like an exasperated kid.

"I mean, how old would you say that 45 is? Forty, fifty years old?"

"Don't do a metaphor."

"No, but what would you say the odds are of that 45 playing as well as it does after all these years?"

"Don't do a metaphor."

"I'm just saying, what are the chances? I'd say that 45 is quite a survivor, like Maxine. What do you think? You going to be the one to break it?"

He closed his eyes and pressed the edge of the vinyl against his forehead. The other hand rested on his bony hip.

"I can't tell you how much I hate it when you do that."

Then he walked over and put the 45 back in its paper jacket. "Look, I'm going to call the cops myself. Tell them what I know."

I was dusting the coffee table with the corner of my robe while assessing his sincerity. "No, you won't."

"Well, hear me when I say if you get into any shit, I'm not going to be the one to drag your ass out of it."

He was cleaning one fingernail with another. I pushed my glasses to my forehead to better rub my sinuses. "Sure you will."

He walked over and sat in the newly positioned easy chair.

We sat very still for a very long time.

"You stole a drunk's car?"

He didn't seem too upset when he asked, just inquisitive. Still, I didn't want to leave him with less than a straightforward answer. Not after lying to him at the club. Not after saying I wasn't going to do what he wanted me to do, regardless. No, the truth was definitely in order.

"I put it back."

He pulled the lever on the side of the chair, which put his feet up for him. I leaned over the arm and kissed him good night before going to bed. He didn't kiss me back, but I thought I heard him say he loved me as I closed the door between us.

10
◇◇◇◇◇◇

When I got up three hours later, Felix was still in the chair snoring. I tried to stay quiet, shuffling toward the kitchen cabinet that housed the Pepto Bismol.

Yeah, I was going to work, but this time I'd be telling my boss that I wouldn't be back. The end. There wasn't enough time in the day to handle both my lives any longer and the bullet-riddled nightmare that held me spellbound had finally won over the security-driven daydream I'd been clinging to for moral support. Felix would have to take up the financial slack while I figured things out. I drove slowly while considering my imminent actions (employment versus unemployment), passing Mi Juanita's Taco Barn, Jelly's Donut Shop, the Texaco and 7-11 I passed every Monday through Friday.

Catching a red light in front of the 7-11, I watched a withered, scabby youth paw at the change returns of all three telephones out front. He kept pulling up his trousers as he rummaged for change. Neither his spirit nor ass seemed robust enough to offer any solid support. Giving up on the phones as a source of income, he dug deep into a pocket while manipulating both rubbery legs back through the double glass doors, and donated a coin to one of the pinball machines inside. The light turned green.

I arrived at the paper about two hours late. As I walked toward my desk, Eve started hollering from across the hall.

"Here already? Hey, everybody, look what the cat dragged in. Look, it's the Queen of England come to grace us with her presence."

The fact that she has nothing clever to say never stops her for a minute. That's the beauty of Eve. My boss came out of his office.

"What happened to you? You all right?"

"No, I'm under the weather. Listen, can I have a word with you sometime this morning?"

"I think you should turn around and go home. Get well. I've had Bill finish up those flyers I needed. Everything's taken care of here, Julie." For the first time, I thought I saw disappointment tucked right behind his professionalism.

"When can I talk to you, sir?"

"I see. Well, I'm on my way to a meeting with the City Manager right now. In fact, I'm running late. We can talk after lunch. That good?"

I thought how this would give me plenty of time to update my resume and gather some office supplies.

"Sure, after lunch is fine. Thank you, sir."

He grabbed his jacket and left. Once the boss was gone, Peterson told me how she felt about the whole thing. Her name is Sally but we all call her by her last name for some reason. Peterson is the boss' secretary and, in my experience, has always shown herself to be both honest and discreet, though her personality is anything but subtle.

"You might want to consider an answering machine, babe. I called three times. Not that I have anything else to do." She fluffed a huge pile of folders on her desk. She's also wonderfully sarcastic.

"Sorry, Peterson."

"Yes, you are. Are you really sick?"

"No."

"Good, because it would be just like you to give me some buggy shit right before my big date tomorrow night."

"Tony?"

"Personals."

"Personals? Where's Tony?"

"I was hoping you knew."

I went through my desk and the cupboards filling my valise to capacity, then gently placed the banjo-playing frog in my purse. I was ready to go but it was only 11:30.

I put my lighter on the desk and spun it around with the eraser end of a pencil. Round and round. Spinning a little too hard, I flung it off the desk, which made a big crash. Eve eyed the twinkling conversation piece. I swooped it up as soon as possible but it was too late. She was already pulling up a chair.

Interestingly, Eve could be telling your boss how incompetent you were one minute and think she was your best friend the next. Right then, she thought we were friends.

"Hey, kiddo. Did you get that from Maxine Montego?"

There are those times in your life when you're hit with something so shocking it's almost like nothing happened at all. Empty space. Hair I was unaware I had stood up on the back of my neck. My eyes glazed over and my lips wouldn't move.

"Juuulieee, did you get that lighter from Maxine Montego?"

She knew it was a lighter. She knew Maxine. I just stared at her blankly.

"You smoke that crack cocaine, don't'cha. You and your beatnik boyfriend smoke the dope, don't'cha. Can you hear me right now? I'll bet you can't even hear me. You've been acting real funny the last few days. And I don't mean funny ha ha, either."

"Eve, how do you know Maxine Montego?"

"Oh! Oh! There you are! Welcome back. How was your trip?"

She was delighted with herself. She was also too close to my face. I grabbed the nondescript collar of her beige blouse. She tried to lean away but couldn't. "Eve, how do you know Maxine Montego?"

"Jesus, Joseph and Mary! Let me go, you hop-head!"

I did. She ran down the hall with her arms stiffly at her sides, mincing her steps like she had diarrhea, heading for the publisher's office. Now it was just Peterson and me. Peterson picked up the slack.

"Julie, lots of people know Maxine Montego. Stop acting like a freak. Did you buy it or did she give it to you?"

The ocean pounded rhythmically in my ears. I decided not to say anything more until I could figure out what was going on. Until then, I would play along.

"Shshshe gave it to me."

"Oh, my God! That's so cool. You actually got a Maxine Montego give-away! Oh, my God. Where was she?"

"Liquor store."

"Not the liquor store where those guys got shot."

"Uh, no."

"Oh, my God! I can't believe it. That's so exciting. What kind of give-away was it? Was she there with the station or was she just hanging out?"

"She... She just ran in for some smokes."

"Wow, you sure happened to be at the right place at the right time."

"That's me in a nutshell."

"Let me see it." She grabbed the lighter out of my hand. "I saw this when she was selling them on the show. God, it's so fierce. It looks so real."

I grabbed it back sooner than I normally would have had I not been feeling so protective.

"Peterson, what radio station does she work for again?"

She cocked her head and moved her ears back, like a dog listening.

"You don't even know who Maxine Montego is, do you?"

Peterson was both honest and discreet. I could go here.

"No."

"I can't believe that you'd get a Maxine Montego give-away and not even know who she is. Only you, Julie."

"Yeah. So..."

"So, freak, Maxine Montego is only the hottest host on the Home Shopping Network. The newspaper tried to do a feature on her once but she said she doesn't do interviews. One time I saw her at the opening of that new Ralph's on Vincent Highway."

"She's a host on the what?"

"The Home Shopping Network. Don't tell me you haven't heard of HSN."

"Yes, I have. I've heard of the Home Shopping Network. We don't have a television, that's all."

"Well, aren't you both just ever so. No answering machine. No TV. Do you churn your own butter?"

"You're hilarious, Peterson. Why is she famous?"

"She's famous because she does these give-aways, like you're holding in your hand, weirdo. She shows up at a premier or, whatever, a liquor store, and gives something away that she's been selling on her show. Usually though, as opposed to you, she gives stuff to fans."

"Fans, right. Why does she do that?"

"She says it makes her feel good. And it makes her very damn popular. I couldn't tell you the name of any other host on HSN. I guess the station didn't like it when she started doing it a few months ago. But then they made so much money off of her, got so many more shoppers, they started to support the idea. That's what I heard. Sometimes she sets time aside on her show just for the give-aways."

I really couldn't follow what the hell Peterson was saying at all. "Does she sing?"

She chuckled as she answered. "I think Eve's right. You're high."

"She doesn't sing?"

"Why would she sing? It's the Home Shopping Network, not the Donny and Marie Show. Nobody sings. They sell stuff. How could you have not heard of it? Maxine sells jewelry mostly, jewelry and face products and shit."

I had this sense that the puzzle pieces were falling into place without me. Like when you're trying to figure out a riddle and someone blurts out the answer right before you get it on your own.

So not only was the woman of the hour well known, she was well known for selling jewelry, not writing songs.

I marveled at how Maxine was somehow able to maintain her anonymity after going underground. Sounded like the whole world knew her and at the same time, nobody did. Sometimes the best place to hide is the most public one.

Television was certainly risky given her more sordid associations. She didn't even change her name, not on the air, not on the cigar boxes. Were her balls really that big or was she, as Felix had suggested, a little tetched in the head?

"When is this show on?"

"Oh, all the time."

"What does that mean, all the time?"

"God, psycho. I think she's on tonight."

"Station?"

"I don't know. You flip it around 'till you find it. You don't have a TV. What are you gonna flip?"

"I'm going to flip you, Peterson."

I grabbed my purse from under the desk and rose to leave. Then, having caught my foot in the shoulder strap of the purse, lassoed myself falling splat to my knees.

Peterson doubled over with glee. The sight gag of the century was hers and hers alone. The pain kept me down for a moment. She eventually came over to help me up. We both leaned against my desk exhausted for different reasons.

"What was she wearing?"

She was obviously fascinated with Maxine. I understood. As I thought about how to answer, I realized that I didn't really know what Maxine looked like. I knew a couple of her songs. I knew a couple of her secrets. Would I recognize her if we were face-to-face again?

After all, the only time I'd actually seen the woman monopolizing my every breath was the night we'd met. I tried to bring her to mind, rubbing the lighter in my pocket.

The image in my head kept changing, tall, short, pretty, spent. Yet she was the most indelible woman in the world. I'd never known anyone so compelling. Why couldn't I describe her? I felt myself drifting into memory consciousness fighting to bring back the moment.

"I only saw her for a second when she went in and a second when she came out. I was outside."

"Did she talk to you? Did she say anything?"

"No."

"Yes, she did. I'm so sure. What did she say?"

"She didn't say anything. Honestly. She looked tired."

"What was she wearing? She's so retro, I swear. She's so chic. I wish I had some of her clothes."

"Yeah, I remember she was very elegant in a skewed sort of way."

"I'm so sure she just gave you that lighter and didn't say anything."

"And she had on a cape, a gray tweed cape. I remember because people don't really wear capes, do they? This one only came down to her butt."

"A cape!"

"And leggings. No, capris. Black capris and a real swank pair of silver shoes with a kitten heel and pointy toe. Oh, and she had these huge sunglasses on at night. I thought that was odd."

"Wow."

"Her painted eyebrows were visible over the top of the black frames. And she had on a beautiful pair of shimmering diamond earrings. They kept twinkling through her tightly coifed hair."

"Cubic zirconium."

"No, auburn. She looked like every woman in every Fellini film."

"I said the earrings were probably cz's, Einstein. Maxine Montego's the queen of cubic zirconium. Why would she wear diamonds? Duh."

"Why wouldn't she?"

"Right. Well, I asked what she was wearing and now I fully know."

"But the thing I remember most clearly is her skin. Weird. Waxy. Have you ever really looked at her skin?"

"Julie, did you fuck her?"

"What?" My reverie had been irreversibly interrupted.

"You're obsessed. It's not natural."

"What did you say?"

"I watch her at least twice a week and I couldn't describe her like that."

"Is that so?"

"Uh, yeah."

"That's because you're cursed with a short attention span, Peterson. Too much television."

"Hello!" Peterson banged her head with the fistfull of files in her hand. "You are a complete psycho freak today, babe. Go home. I gotta take this disk to Circulation. You can keep describing her if you want." Peterson waved a little wave on her way out the door.

Apparently, I remembered what she looked like. I remembered her weak hands, her sad mouth. I remembered that she smelled like money, and gin. I remembered that I wanted to protect her and run from her the moment she got out of that big black car. Funny, all this exposition later, I felt exactly the same way.

11
◆◆◆◆◆◆◆

I was a girl on a mission. Tired of observing this espionage from shadows and hearsay, answers were necessary now. I didn't know what to say to her but I knew that my next conversation would be with Maxine Montego, directly. I raced across town, streetlights tumbling off of the hood of my polished black Saab, window down, radio up.

The sky filled with ominous, low-slung clouds making it mighty dark for the middle of the afternoon, and there was a chill that suggested rolling the window up but I ignored the suggestion.

I raced through the hills and inappropriate darkness noticing for a second time how deceptively lovely Berle looked down there.

You get far enough away from anything and it inevitably looks a butt-load better (or worse) than it does up close, but from a distance things never, ever appear as they really are. Maybe that's why I keep my distance from most everybody. Because I know if I can keep you far enough away, I'll look like a regular gal. Not even Felix can appreciate how many ghosts travel with me everywhere I go. My brain is a constant clog of pins and worms and every day I make it through undetected is an effort and victory.

I had buried Ms. Hyde a long time ago but I could feel her pulling on my sleeve. I could hear her whispering through the speakers of my radio. I could see her reflection in my bathroom mirror.

I tried to take my life once. One more awkward attempt at self-expression. Why? One day it just hit me that I'd been kidding myself. I wasn't Kafka. I wasn't even Jacqueline Suzanne. I talked about writing more than I actually wrote. I hung out at local bookshops listening to authors read excerpts from their latest best-sellers, stalking them as they made their way to the coffee bar, then cars, like some creep begging for a restraining order. I subscribed to writers' magazines so I could see them sitting on my coffee table, proving who and what I was to myself each time I dusted them.

I was obsessed with being a writer, not with writing. And when you're truly obsessed with something, you want to do more than understand it. You want to be it, to lay it, to ingest it. To convince the world you are it, not the aped, dingy double you actually are.

And with that flash of insight, I stopped caring about everything. No artistic goals that looked even vaguely attainable, no further visions of glory, no one to become.

Once an artist realizes they might actually die unrecognized, there is a common, albeit pathetic, attempt at absolution that goes, "It's not about fame or money or love, man. It's about the process." Next time you hear some creative type say something like that, stick a fork in his eye.

So I crawled into the tub and jammed a disposable

steel blade into my wrist thinking I'd found a way around the burden of expectation. Better I should kill myself than let disappointment have the pleasure. But killing yourself is harder than you might realize. And as I stumbled around the bathroom clutching my wounds, I knew for fact what I wouldn't admit to a soul. Whatever actual potential I possessed was handcuffed to the counter of the local drug store.

My affinity for pills had both sharpened and scrambled my writing abilities over the years, but slitting my wrist was just so pitiful and badly executed I felt nothing but embarrassed as my blood stained the bathroom tile. It was then I considered easing up on the medication.

It took about a year to get clean. Once sober, I floated from job to job in search of something other than drugs and aspirations to anchor me. Then I met Felix.

It wasn't fair, what I put on him. I saw him as some kind of incomprehensible wunderkind. But that's how obsessive people are, if not one thing, then another. I was focused again. I was fixated. Things were looking up. And as infatuation possessed me completely, my individuality, however twisted to begin with, started to disintegrate. No need for it anymore. I could identify myself through him. Strangely enough, he started getting great gigs, lots of press. He's a horn player, not a rock star. But somehow, my manic intensity was so powerful, I actually shifted the earth's gravitational pull and he became as close to a rock star as a horn player can be. Maybe he would've done just as well without me but this is how it seemed.

I didn't care. Oxygen once again filled my lungs

and I clung to him as life support throughout my creativity coma, a coma I only began to come out of in the weeks prior to that Cadillac pulling up at the Liquor Palace. When that Cadillac pulled up, everything changed. I began to breathe on my own.

Obsession raised its impish head, coughed out the cobwebs, and blew a serious dose of high-octane fairy dust right in my face. And this time, love didn't manipulate the circumstance. This time I could suck the energy out of my new host, feeding off her situation, finally getting stronger.

Maxine Montego reanimated my imagination like heaven's alarm clock at the end of a dark sleep. She was a peep show offering everything that made me breathe hard: pain, loss, regret, greasy characters, seedy deals, and an irresistible talent. She teased me till all my nickels were gone. She was caffeine. Benzedrine. A mythological speedball coursing through my ready veins. And danger played no small part in my nearly libidinous need to pry into the warped vinyl of this singer's life.

A balanced life was neither in my past nor future. I'm not convinced that anything profound or even mildly entertaining has ever come of a balanced life anyway. I'd located my edge and was standing on it for the first time in a long time. I didn't give a shit about anything else.

Piecing together all these thoughts and motivations for the first time, I found myself thanking a god I wasn't sure I believed in for giving me this most golden opportunity, this thrilling adventure.

Then I pondered that the process might actually be the point, after all.

I turned onto her street of onyx asphalt and emerald green lawns. No sidewalks to divide the two predominant colors I couldn't see the last time I'd dropped by. In the oddly dim light of day, these homes were even more impressive. Magazine beautiful. Hollywood in the thirties.

When I saw the sprawling ranch house, I pulled over one estate short of my destination, lit a cigarette, and watched. I thought about walking up to that big Spanish door, then I lit another cigarette.

Almost thirty minutes later the front door opened. She and Peter walked out.

For a seventy-plus-year-old woman, Maxine was so fine.

She wore a leopard print swing coat and indigo sharkskin capris. Her hair looked like fire, blazing darkly from around the red chiffon scarf attempting to contain it. This was the same scarf, I romanticized, that had been on the back seat of her Cadillac the night we met.

Peter had a felt hat on his head like he'd worn the night of the murders, and a handsome wool overcoat that made him look a little taller than I remembered. In fact, he didn't look so bad. His face was lined and leathery but almost rugged from where I sat. The shadow had lifted.

They looked perfect together. A couple of casual swells stuck in the wrong calendar year. He had one hand on her back and the other supporting a small suitcase. Arms crossed tightly in front of her, she looked at the bizarre sky and then the ground while walking to the car.

As Peter bent to unlock her door, Maxine turned on instinct. She looked right at me as if I'd called her name. She said nothing to Peter as he threw the suitcase in the back and held out his hand for hers. But as she carefully climbed in, he too, looked my way.

How do you follow someone who knows you're following them? I'm not the one to ask. All I could do was start the engine and make a U-turn to fall in behind them.

So, there we were driving our two shiny black knockouts down the winding street. Looked like a small funeral procession.

They weren't driving fast. I had time, this time, to take in the jarring transition from scenic splendor to the small stretch of industry you pass through at the bottom of the hill. It's funny how different things can be block to block.

Apex Steel and Shorty's Automatic Screw Machine, Bert's Brown and Sharp and Chan's Big Burger were all open for business as they had been since God knows when.

Peter and Maxine talked heatedly all the way downtown, hands flapping, fingers pointing. Peter glanced in his rear view mirror more than once, eventually turning onto 5th Street. Then, maybe one block past Esther, he pulled over and stopped the car.

I didn't know what to do. I certainly hadn't been clever about following them but I knew I couldn't just pull over, so I rolled by them at a snail's pace. I passed Roberta Avenue, then Bartelle. Then I gave up being coy and turned around.

The Cadillac had pulled over in front of Romeo and Juliet's Custom Tailoring. Their heads followed mine as I subtly passed them again, this time going in the opposite direction.

If I'd been driving an army tank with a piano strapped to it, I couldn't have been any more conspicuous. I sheepishly pulled into the parking lot to the left of the shoeshine stand.

The guy who shines shoes was out front doing so. He waved at me. I waved back, feeling mighty dumb. I kept my chin up by telling myself that he didn't know how stupid I was.

By the time I turned the car around so as to be facing the street exit of this usually busy dirt parking lot, the Cadillac pulled in to join me.

Peter got out and headed my way. He slid his hand inside his open coat and kept it there as he approached. Ironically, my headache lifted for the first time in days.

Maxine was three steps behind him sauntering toward me. When she called out, he stopped but kept his hand where it was. She passed him grumbling, "Really, Peter. Honestly." He begrudgingly retracted his hopefully idle threat.

She stood directly in front of my window. When the sunglasses came off, she bent down to lock me in a reciprocal gaze.

I had never seen such an extraordinary face. One eye was real, one eye was not. The variation between them, immeasurable but apparent. They were olive green. Her waxy skin looked like it might crack, if dropped. She was gorgeous and macabre, friendly and foreboding. I didn't want to stare at her skin so I tried to look her in the eye. But which one?

"Hello." Her voice was as deep and dark as her secrets. She made no move to shake my hand. I made no move at all.

"I'm Maxine Montego."

"I know," I whispered.

"I see. Well, that puts me at a rather awkward disadvantage, doesn't it?"

"Julie Page," I reported, sounding like an automaton all of a sudden. Peter shifted from foot to foot as I cleared my throat.

"Hello, Miss Page. This is my friend, Edward G. Robinson."

Maxine gestured toward Peter who rolled his eyes while readjusting his hat. She almost smiled.

"Have we met?"

"I'm a big fan of yours."

"How nice."

There was a deafening silence for several heartbeats.

"You're not a private investigator, are you, Miss Page?"

"No. No, nothing like that."

"I'm joking. Your tailing skills are, shall we say, limited?"

"Oh. Yes. Yes, ma'am, they are."

"What can we do for you, Miss Page? I can't help but think there's something you're terribly serious about pursuing here. What is it? Autograph? Directions, perhaps?"

"You've written so many incredible songs, it's just an honor."

Her shock was notable. Straightening herself slowly she smoothed out her cheeks, smoothed them out from mouth to ears, as she considered my compliment.

"My my, you are a fan."

"I'm a writer."

She went very still when I said that. Ten China red

talons tapped down on the plastic inside casing of my surprised car door.

"Tell me, are you a good writer? Would I know your work?"

Staring past her, I muttered, "Those are two very different questions."

She laughed. It looked like it hurt.

"Yes, they certainly are. Would you excuse me for a moment?"

Obviously, I would excuse her quite a lot. She took a step toward Peter as he took a step toward her. She laid her hands on his lapels. I couldn't make out everything she was saying but whatever it was, Peter didn't like it one bit.

"Oh, that's priceless, Max," he shouted, pushing his hat back on his head.

He grabbed her forearm. She started to pull away. He grabbed the other forearm and pulled her to his chest. Her bony fists were now positioned an inch from his mug, because he'd positioned them there.

He issued his two cents 'till he'd thrown in at least five bucks nose-to- nose with his nemesis. All I could make out was, "something... blow it, Max... something, something...not now... something...done with this shit." Then he pushed her away like he was real done. She slapped him. I bet it hurt her hand more than his cheek. This guy had been slapped before. He rubbed his neck. She turned away.

"Miss Page, as fate would have it, I happen to be in the market for a writer. I'm wondering if you would be good enough to drive me to my destination this evening so that we might discuss the possibility of a collaboration. Would you mind?"

I peed myself a little.

Peter was at her shoulder pad. "Kid, if anything funny happens, anything at all, I'm going to blow your brains out." He wasn't yelling, he was explaining.

"Pete's opposed to the idea." She shook her head at the wind as I'd seen her do before. My mouth opened but no sound came out.

Peter started to walk away but she hailed him down one more time. "Peter, the makeup case, would you get it?"

He brought it over and handed it to me through the window.

"This is so sloppy, Maxine. So unnecessary."

"And Peter, remember I'm going back on during Kevin's show tonight. I won't be ready for the car until some time after that. I don't know when he'll be able to have me on."

"Aren't we expecting company tonight?"

"When I call. When we're home."

"I'll be there at midnight. If I have to wait, I'll wait."

He looked at her hard while straightening his tie. "Is she going to drive you to work or am I gonna leave you stranded in a dirt lot?"

"What do you say, Miss Page? Shall we dance?"

I couldn't begin to imagine why she was about to get in my car but I wasn't going to question it. I got out and opened the door for her, buttoning the collar of my army surplus coat and straightening my glasses.

He fished out his keys ignoring me completely. "Be careful, Max."

"I will, Peter. I'll be very careful," she said, sincerely.

As he started the car, he gave Maxine a last 'Why are you doing this?' look. Her back was to me as we both watched him pull out onto 5th.

"Goodbye, Peter," she said quiety.

Maxine remained facing the alley long after the Cadillac disappeared. I had questions but pushing her didn't seem wise. Besides, I was so nervous, I could hardly remember how to talk.

Then I noticed her shoulders shaking. They were shaking real hard. I started to panic as she finally turned her attention to me.

"Miss Montego?"

This was the face of despair. The saddest face I've ever seen. Three hundred and sixty degrees from the calm and authority she exuded a moment before. Emotion clogged her eyes making one look as glassy as the other. When the tears fell, they bounced off her face like rain off a freshly Armoralled landau top.

"Oh, Maxine," I thought, "don't go goofy on me now."

12

◇◇◇◇◇◇◇

"Don't touch me. I can do this. I can do this, goddamnit."

"Do what?" I was waiting for an answer that
would never come from her.

She carefully dabbed at her face with a handkerchief exhumed from one of those huge pockets, shook
her head again, and walked over to the passenger side
of my car as if it never happened. The sky made with
a scary growl making us both look up.

"Looks like rain," I said.

"I do love the wind," she said.

She picked up the makeup case from the passenger seat and placed it in her lap as the door closed.
How much makeup does it take to get a woman to
look like that? Through all the waterworks, not one
smear of mascara sullied her science-fiction eyes, not
one tear-furrowed streak parted her rouge.

She reached into the other pocket, this time producing a cigarette case worthy of attention. It was a
dark antiqued gold and on the far left of the lid three
large jade leaves surrounded a very substantial ruby,
as garish and stunning as its owner.

"Do you mind if I smoke?"

I aimed the barrel of my lighter at her and pulled the trigger. She glared at it, never once looking over at me, and slowly passed two fingers through the flame. As if my own fingers had been singed, I jerked the lighter a few inches back but she gently cupped her fingers around mine pulling the flame close enough to light her cigarette.

After a long drag, she repositioned herself to face me. "I thought we'd met before."

What an idiot I am. I could've used a match.

Lighting a cigarette of my own, I looked out the window uncertain what to say about our prior meeting. I tried this. "Thanks for the give-away, Miss Montego. I use it all the time."

She dropped her lids half-mast. Her version of a squint, I figure. "Are you a fan of my show as well as my music, Miss Page?"

"Who isn't?"

"Mmm. Well, in the years I've been with the show, no one has ever mentioned my music. Not once. Seems no one has made the connection. That earmarks you as quite a serious fan. Or something."

"Huh."

"Anyway, I've sent Peter on a rather lengthy, impromptu errand, and I don't actually have to be at the studio for a while, so we have some time to get acquainted."

"Great. Where would you like to go?"

She exhaled a smoky chuckle. "Nowhere in particular. You know what they say about a moving target."

Her eyes twinkled as she tried to feel out just how much I knew but I wasn't going to tell her and she wasn't going to help.

"Actually, Miss Page, let's go to the boardwalk, if you don't mind. I've always loved it there."

I decided not to push it. Time would tell even if Maxine wouldn't.

"Is that cigarette case real?" I asked, in an attempt to breathe life into the dead air.

"No. It only exists for those who believe."

Her jibe embarrassed me.

"Forgive me if I'm not terribly amusing today, Miss Page. Sometimes, I'm awfully funny. The case is real in every respect. Eighteen-carat gold, real stones, Lucky Strikes. It walks like it talks."

"I thought it might be an elaborate replica given your line of work."

"No, it's not. Sometimes a cigar is just a cigar."

I could feel my ears get hot. Was she baiting me to say something about the smuggling? I wasn't ready.

"Sometimes it's almost impossible to distinguish that which is authentic from that which is less than authentic. Do you shop with us often, Miss Page?"

"Shop?"

"With the Home Shopping Network."

"Oh. Right. No. But I've been meaning to." She was making me pick at my cuticles. "Gosh, 'Closer to the Hip' is such a brilliant song. I can't believe I'm sitting with the woman who wrote it."

Her stare softened as she butted out what remained of her smoke.

"My God, 'Closer to the Hip.' No, it isn't a brilliant song, but thanks for saying so." She started to wax gloomy again. "How comic."

"What?"

"How comic that I'd be paid a compliment like that today."

"What about today?"

Her impossibly heavy lashes fluttered as she chose a reply. "Nothing. People never bring up my music, that's all. I don't travel in those circles anymore. My fans today have no idea who I was."

"Who you are."

"Please. Who I was. And, while we're on it, how do you know anything about my music? You're much too young and it's not easy to find."

"My boyfriend is a musician. He turned me on to it."

"Musician. You've got your hands full. What does he play?"

"Felix plays the sax."

"Felix?" she said, incredulously. "Felix Mint?"

I thought I was about to have an orgasm or a stroke. I couldn't tell which. The most extraordinarily hot tingle ran through me and my hands went completely numb. When I could control my tongue, I asked the obvious question. "How do you know my boyfriend?"

"Liner notes. I'm voracious about liner notes. He's a very solid player."

Overwhelmed with pride as well as that uncomfortable pang that strikes whenever I'm left to ponder what such a celebrated guy is doing with the likes of me, I sat mute for what seemed like days. Worthlessness and insecurity began to cloud my mission. I could feel it happening and I had no time for it. This doesn't belong to Felix I told myself in a hurry. This is yours. Don't fuck up. Say something.

"You're a legend, Miss Montego. Don't underestimate your influence on God knows how many artists – including Felix Mint."

Her lip quivered and her eyes misted over. "I'll take that with me."

Take it with her where? When I thought about the possibilities, prison among them, her words took on an even greater sadness.

"Miss Page, I've recently considered hiring someone to handle my memoirs. Would you be willing to take that on?"

Could the day get any weirder?

"Miss Page?"

"Uh, yes. Yes, I'm willing to try."

"Timing has worked to your advantage today, Miss Page."

"Look, I don't want to talk you out of this but just because I'm a writer, doesn't mean I'm a good one. I haven't written anything in quite awhile."

"Darling, I don't have time to shop. Are you a writer?"

"Yeah, I am. It's just…" There went my tongue.

I averted my rapidly batting lids, glancing first at the steering wheel then back at her, but I couldn't seem to look any higher than her neck. After considering my lost expression, Maxine decided to take another line of questioning.

"Tell me, how far do you think you'd be willing to go to get the job done?"

"I don't know. Pretty far, I think."

Her eyes continued to burn a hole in the side of my sweaty head.

"I'm not trying to bond with you, Miss Page. I need to know before I take you somewhere you don't belong. Let's pretend that this is the most important question anyone will ever ask you. Let's say that everything in your life is riding on this one. Now, let me ask you again. Are you willing to take this on?"

She was scaring the shit out of me. Not because I was afraid of what I might be getting into but because she could be really scary. I was bobbing my head up and down and my mouth was open but so far, no response.

She threw her head back and her eyes to the heavens then stared out the windshield as if she'd given up.

"Yes, I am," I finally managed.

She softened and relaxed as she turned her waxy face back in my direction. "Are you sure? You seem more like a mime than a writer. Are you a mime?"

That broke the tension for me. I actually chuckled. "No, ma'am, I'm a writer."

"Good. Now art is a dirty business if you're any good at it. Are you good at your craft, Marcel? Just nod your head."

"Yes, ma'am, as I recall, I am."

"Mmm. Well, you have just enough damage on your face to keep me from dismissing that answer as bullshit."

"Thanks, I think. It's just that you don't know anything about me. I've been going through some heavy changes lately and…"

"Jesus Christ. That's fascinating. Let's cut the crap, shall we? I'm not sure, nor do I care, what your other motivations are, but I'm fairly certain that the primary reason you've been following me, however long that's been, is to get a story out of it. And I may have one for you."

Wow. Maybe she was right. "I don't normally follow people. Forgive me."

She lit up like a giant marquee. "Perhaps I have the power to inspire you, sweetheart, but I'm not quite omnipotent enough to wash away your sins."

"I'd take inspiration over absolution any day."

Raising her arched penciled brows she swiveled her jaw from side to side. Then the old woman said, "I can dig that," which sounded pretty damn natural coming out of her, like maybe she'd invented the phrase.

"Are we ready?"

"Ready to what?"

"To drive."

"Oh, sure." I turned the ignition and made my way to the street. "So, how are we going to do this?"

"What?"

"Collaborate on your book."

"We're doing it now."

"Yes, but when can we work out an interview schedule?"

"Darling, no schedule. This is it."

We were barely moving as I had lifted my foot from the gas, not sure if I should pull over or keep going. I couldn't catch a red light to save my ass.

"What do you mean this is it?"

"Do you have a tape recorder?"

"No, I don't have a tape recorder."

"You should always have a tape recorder with you."

"Okay, but I don't."

"Well then, I guess you're just going to have to remember our conversation and do your homework."

"Are you telling me this is the only time we're going to talk?"

"Yes, I'm afraid so. Big projects bore me."

"And from this, you expect me to write a book?"

"You're losing that awestruck feeling, aren't you?"

"I can't do that. Nobody could do that."

The car ambled down 5th as I tried to decide whether to pull over or drive. "Where am I supposed to be going?"

She leaned her head against the car window. "The boardwalk." Sitting up a little straighter, she turned back toward me. "So, what shall we talk about, Miss Page?"

This must have been how Peter felt, bulldozed. Even though I was convinced this would not be the only interview session, she was there and willing to talk so I embraced the moment.

"Okay, why don't you think 'Closer to the Hip' is a brilliant song?"

"Because I've written brilliant songs. I know the difference. Next."

"Uh, how many songs have you written?"

"This isn't going to be a very good book, is it?"

I finally hit the gas hard. The sun was trying to poke through the clouds. In those seconds of silence, we both pulled out our smokes again. I lit mine. She lit hers. Every woman for herself. She made me mad and she made me nervous. And I really wanted her to like me. I calmly asked myself what would the world want to know about Maxine Montego?

"Okay. How did you get here from where you started?"

She ran her hands across the top of the makeup case and then from her cheeks to her ears.

"Now that, Miss Page, is a very good question."

13

◇◇◇◇◇◇◇

She carefully put the case under her feet like a little ottoman. She was so small. It still fascinates me that someone can, by sheer weight of personality, appear to be three times larger than they are.

"How much do you know about me? Did that musician of yours tell you any checkered stories?"

"He told me about the fire, if that's what you mean."

"I see. Did Felix Mint tell you that I'm crazy?" A sly grin cheated its way across her mouth.

"Miss Montego, why don't you tell me what happened that night."

She pulled off the chiffon scarf and threw it on the dash. After rearranging her oxblood-colored synthetic locks, she produced a bottle of pills from a pocket. The lid came off easily with one turn of her mechanical wrist. She delicately placed a tablet on her tongue and swallowed.

"Yes, let me tell you about that."

All at once, there was a stoic clip to the way she spoke.

"Got to the club a half hour before the first set, as usual. Harry was behind the bar, as usual. I had on a beret, long black turtleneck masquerading as a dress, black fishnet stockings, and yellow patent leather boots. The boots were a gift. I was going through a brief 'mod' period."

"Well, it was 1967, right?"

"My, you have done some homework. You know, someone actually took a picture of me in them. I've still got it. An Iowa housewife who happened to be there the night I caught on fire took my picture and made a copy for me."

"Oh, God."

"She didn't know. She and her husband had left before the real floorshow began. When they got back home, she sent it to the club for me as a little treasure. Harry didn't know what to do with it so he sent it to the hospital. There I am, shattered hands, broken collar bone, hair gone, eye gone, two thirds of my skin gone, and I get this ridiculous picture delivered to me with a note that says, 'Love the boots.'"

"That's brutal."

"I kept the image of my former self at my bedside for months in the hospital. I was haunted by it. I mean, was it a directive or an opinion? Love the boots."

She waited until she was sure I got the joke then continued.

"The crowd was friendly. The boys were sober and on time. I was flattered to be asked to sing a song of mine called 'Nobody's Fool' but chose to open with 'Lovers Lane' instead. We did a ten-song set. Turn here."

I turned.

"We took a break. I had a drink. Next set, I opened with 'Nobody's Fool.'

In the middle of the second verse, I saw smoke by the dining room. Then tiny gold flickers, then flames. It happened in an instant, racing in both directions. The blue velvet draped along the walls seemed to guide the flames until all at once we were encased. Absolutely breathtaking."

"Are you saying you could've warned everyone before it spread?"

"Probably."

"So, why didn't you?"

"I was singing!" she howled, then immediately regained her composure.

"I was singing. No one seems to have maintained any respect at all for the show going on anymore. The show goes on, goddamnit."

I thought about how stupid that sounded, how ludicrous it would be to cripple yourself for the sake of what? A song? Then I thought how, more than likely, she'd already had that conversation with herself.

"Your dedication was harshly rewarded."

"Mmm. The boys were getting antsy anyway. I suppose it was time for us all to move on."

"There are less dramatic ways to break up a band."

"True enough. Here we are. Turn right."

We parked on the backside of the boardwalk and stared at the rear wall behind the bumper cars. Heavy oak slats creaked gently beneath us.

"At first, people were confused and trying to collect their belongings. Burning debris began to drizzle then rain on the crowd. That's when the screaming started. People jumping over one another, struggling to get to the only available exit. Not easy when you've been drinking."

"You remember everything so clearly."

"Every moment in freeze-frame. I saw a woman grab another woman's hair trying to swing her out of the way but a clump of bloody scalp came out mid-swing. I saw a fellow hit his girl with a closed fist knocking her out so he could carry her without a fight. I saw one of my band mates grab his axe and use it like a battering ram, bashing his way to the door. And I watched the liquor explode, one bottle at a time. First, shattering glass, then combustion. Liquid Roman Candles, each wet trail carrying the fire further into the room. That was its own little thrill show. So many pretty, colorful bottles. Come to find out, the joint was more of a theatre set than a club. Hollow plastic columns and paper-maché frames that appeared to be solid wood were crinkling up in front of me like cellophane. And, of course, many people were on fire, their hair, their clothes, their skin. It's different than in the movies. There's a smell involved."

The windows were down but I wanted more air.

"My drummer ran into me so hard that it propelled me right off the stage and onto a front row table. I was still clenching the microphone. Knocked the wind out of me but I got to my feet."

"What happened...What, uh..." I was pointing to her undilated peeper.

"Drumstick."

"Oh, my God. Was it an accident?"

She gave me a dirty look. "No. He came at me through the flames shouting his disagreement over the tempo of the last number and impaled me."

"Sorry. So then what?"

"So while cradling my half-emptied socket with

my broken hands, I watched flames crawl up my arm. Didn't even feel it, just watched it. Next thing I knew, I was alone in a white room and the morphine wasn't working. No encore that night."

"And the band?"

"I never saw them again."

"That's indefensible."

"That's show biz."

I shook my head at her emotionless rendition of the event. "How can you be so glib about it?"

"For the first two years or so, the pain was fairly preoccupying. When the horror of what I looked like had me hunched over a toilet bowl vomiting out any remaining pride I'd been harboring before the fire, I knew I was healing. Then anger, then glib."

"What finally helped you get over it?"

"What makes you think I'm over it?"

"It was forty years ago. Aren't you?"

"Miss Page, I hope that each of the gentlemen I employed, every musician I gave the honor of playing the most innovative music they'd ever have the opportunity to play, I sincerely hope that each mother fucker who let me lay in that club until my face was gone dies or died a slow, humiliating death. Cowardly, mercenary bastards, all of them. Great band though. Let's walk."

While processing that bit of insight, I walked around to get her door. She got out with the makeup case in tow.

"Miss Montego, why don't we leave it in the car?"

"No, darling, I'll carry it."

"Here, I've got it."

Begrudgingly, she allowed me to take the case from her. I placed it securely under my arm.

We walked between the bumper cars and hot-dog-on-a-stick stand making our way to the boardwalk proper. As twilight landed, bulbs twinkled on. First the Ferris wheel, then Tilt-A-Whirl and so on. The sky grew funky again, its dangerous possibilities now masked by the oncoming night.

"Miss Page, would you mind?" She was referring to the photo booth out front of the arcade.

"No, go ahead."

She pulled two bucks from a money clip and handed them to me. "Would you feed them in?" I did.

"You get in first. I'll stand."

I was speechless. I didn't figure me in the picture. Upon twirling the seat up to accommodate, I mounted it without comment. She wedged herself behind me, only bending a little at the waist to place her face near mine. When they developed, she handed them to me.

"For the dust jacket," she winked.

We walked along the ocean side, watching the crowd thicken along with the darkness. The sea mist wreaked havoc with my hair, not hers, as we watched young hoods and Dairy Queen counter help throw away good money at the balloon shoot and clown toss. I bought some cotton candy.

"You know, Miss Page, I did have one visitor in the hospital. My piano player came by eventually. When he heard the rumor that I was in a county hospital, he came to see if it was true."

"What was that like?"

"Well, up until the fire we had been lovers so I had

a couple of questions I felt justified in asking. For instance, why did he leave me to burn?"

"And his response?"

"During the scene at the club, he looked for me outside. When the ambulance finally came and they pulled what was left of me out of there, they told him there was no way I was going to make it. Apparently, that was good enough for him. Very easily convinced fellow, my pianist, my lover. I'd say he must've wanted out of the relationship pretty badly for it to be that easy to walk away, but he'd never admit to that. Anyway, about a week later, he heard differently.

"Did you ever forgive him?"

"No, but sometimes I feel mildly vindicated when I see the guilt on his tortured face, every time he looks at mine."

I leaned against the wooden octopus in front of the Lite O' Line and looked at her squarely. "Are you talking about Peter?"

She nodded. "In his day he was a wonderful musician. The best accompanist I ever had. He could second-guess my every breath, until I really needed him, of course."

"You went back to him?"

"Honey, I was a mummy suspended by pulleys over a hospital bed. When he found me, I couldn't move let alone leave him. We shared a house, the one you circle every so often, so why upset the program? I needed 24-hour care when they let me go home six months later. Who better to wipe my ass than Peter?"

I was stunned silent by her candor but quickly regrouped.

"How was it after that?"

"We were never intimate again, if you call sex being intimate."

She looked over her shoulder and into the crowd as we passed Madame Vanya's. I did the same, reflexively.

"So many things keep people attached to one another. Unfortunately, it's not always love. For many years he was under the impression that I was going to go back to the stage. He kept pushing me to write."

"Why didn't you?"

She unbuttoned her coat so as to pull it more tightly around her.

"I wanted to but every time he pushed, my talent seemed to burrow a little further underground. I did try for a while then I just stopped. Truth is I was scared for the first time in my artistically courageous life. And I was so tired.

"Felix couldn't see that?"

She jerked her head my way then repositioned it forward without commenting on my Freudian slip.

"I mean, couldn't Peter see that you were too beat up to try again?"

"We see what we choose to see." She considered me somberly. "You're all hung up on that brilliant horn player of yours, aren't you?"

"Well, he is fairly awesome."

"I'll bet all the girls think so."

I stopped to clear my hand of the cotton candy so I could light up. "He never brings it home."

"Good for him. I always did. Peter just looked the other way. Not out of forgiveness or stupidity but rather because he needed me around. I fulfilled what he was missing in himself."

I didn't bother telling her how well I understood that.

She gently tugged at her artificial bangs then wiped the corners of her mouth with a delicate pinkie. "But, for the record, when we were friends it seemed to me that we were the best of friends."

"You're not sure?"

"I'm not sure of anything. Anyway, that was many years ago. When he realized that I wasn't going back on stage, he pulled further and further away until he wasn't there at all."

"Figuratively."

"Right. He still changes the sheets and does the shopping. He's too self-righteous to ever actually leave me."

Again, she turned to see what was behind her.

"Everything okay, Miss Montego?"

"Yes. I think so. Let me carry the makeup case."

"I've got it."

"Give me the case."

I complied.

"Let's head back to the car, shall we?"

We resumed our walk. Her voice remained steady but she was becoming increasingly nervous. Over what, I wasn't sure but I kept talking and we kept moving.

"So what did you do after you healed?"

"The John Tracy Clinic offered me a job recording books for the blind, my voice being my only marketable asset. Job opportunities are limited when you're grotesque. Frankly, I needed the work and it was good to be back in the studio."

"You're not grotesque."

"I am. Trust me."

"How long did you do that?"

"More than a decade. Peter stopped doing sessions when I started working again claiming he wouldn't play until I sang. Asshole. Perfectly wonderful piano player."

"Was he your accompanist when you played the Sahara?"

"Christ, Page, have you already written a book about me?"

"Felix told me about it."

"Felix Mint has a big fat mouth. Have you mentioned that to him?"

"I will."

She clutched her collar for additional warmth and picked up her pace.

I caught up to her, giving an apologetic nod to the kid extending the plastic long-stem rose my way. "Only two dollars, lady." He flicked a switch and the rose lit up.

"Next time," I promised.

As we passed the taffy shop, she resumed the conversation.

"Felix Mint told you about Vegas?"

"Yeah."

"How did he know about that?"

"It's part of your mythology. He said the loss about killed you. That you never really got over it."

"How the hell does he know about my loss? Nobody knew about the baby."

I stopped and by doing so, she knew in an instant that I didn't know anything about a baby. Her expression turned a little clownish, like she'd just received a pie in the face.

"That's not what you were alluding to?"

"I heard that you lost a standing gig to Louis Prima. Pneumonia, or something. That you almost died."

"Well," she shook her head at the sky and continued across the wooden slats to the car. "I did almost die."

"I'm so sorry. What happened?"

"Who am I to amend my mythology? For the book, pneumonia will do just fine."

"Miss Montego, please, who was the father?"

"Elvis. Get this door for me, would you?" I did, dejectedly. "May I continue?"

I started the car and slowly moved onto the main drag.

"When I was recording books, I found myself home quite a bit more than when I was singing. I took to watching a lot of television. In the early eighties, I think it was, I discovered the Home Shopping Network, merely the Home Shopping Club back then."

I tried to hide my frustration but that accidental bit of exposition kept distracting me. "What did you say?"

She tried to drop the corners of her mouth into a pout. "You're sore, aren't you?"

"Disappointed."

"You know, the longer people know me, the more disappointed they become. I'll disappoint you again, Miss Page. It's inevitable."

"You must understand how important it would be to the integrity of your story to talk about a lost baby. Surely, you understand that."

"Darling, God knows what all Felix Mint told you. Sounds like you can't shut him up. But my course was set long before the Sahara."

"How so?"

She checked her watch. "Turn left at this stop, then left again, get us back on track."

"This is a joke, right? That I'm not going to see you again? Tell me you're joking."

Gravely, she responded, "Not this time."

"Miss Montego, I'm starting to panic."

"Yes, I know what you mean."

She popped another pill and lit another smoke, pensive for the first time in my presence.

"Okay, so, how did you get this job I'm driving you to?"

"Right, that's where we were." She rocked gently back and forth, like kids do sometimes.

"My television watching tended to be late in the evening. Hours I was used to working, two, three o'clock in the morning. Sitting dormant in front of the Home Shopping Club became ritual for me. It kept me company. Then one night there was a product introduced called Second Skin; an oil-based foundation accompanied by a brush-on breathable latex topcoat designed to hide any scarring, anything at all. I took a chance and made the call."

"That's what that is?" I gestured to her skin. "Some kind of rubber?"

"I look fabulous, don't I?"

"You look a hell of a lot younger than you are."

"Yes, younger, and very, very odd."

We shared a laugh.

"Here, turn into that alley."

I turned. "So you bought the Second Skin and, then what?"

"I couldn't believe how completely the product covered my quilted, skin-grafted puss. So, I called in one night when it was being demonstrated and gave my testimonial over the air. Turn back onto Hoover."

"Left or right?"

"Right. The host asked me to stay on the line and when they broke away for a station-identification, she asked if I would be willing to be part of an info-mercial for the product."

"Because of who you were?"

"No one gave a shit who I was, but they were awfully impressed with the dramatic difference Second Skin made over scars as sincere as mine. And of course, they loved my voice."

"Of course."

"Soon, I did an infomercial on my own interviewing other stapled beauties. It went over very well. They offered me my own slot. I'd sell Second Skin and other skin care, perfume, candles, you name it. I started selling jewelry about a year later. No one even brought up my sad saga after a while. And though I had sworn I'd never perform in front of an audience again, there I was. And I dug it."

"What about the give-aways?"

"Oh, those. I'm vain. I like being popular, Miss Page. When I first started giving things away on the air it was on a whim. Somebody would call in for something and I would simply give it away."

"How did the studio take that?"

"Not well, I'm afraid. But sales just went through the roof. Eventually, not given much choice, the studio sanctioned the idea. I made sure I had something in my pocket wherever I went. Fans loved it. I loved it. It was such a kick. Made me feel better about things. Still does."

"That's why you gave me the lighter a few nights ago in front of the Liquor Palace?"

I had to broach the subject somehow. My attempt was unproductive. All I accomplished was disrupting her happy memory with a much less happy one. You could tell. She directed me into a lot guarded by two security guys and a big iron gate. It was nearing six o'clock.

"Good evening, Miss Montego. Mr. Common all right?" One guard spoke, the other leaned in and checked things out.

"Hello, Curtis. Peter will be by to pick me up later. Had to run an errand. This is Julie Page. She's just going to drive me to my trailer."

"Have a good show, ma'am." The gate opened and I rolled forward.

I wanted to tell her that I knew about the smuggling and the murders and everything, that maybe I could help if she'd tell me how, but I didn't. She had plenty on her mind already. Would it be cops or thugs she would ultimately answer to? Would it be tonight or tomorrow? Things like that.

I parked. She looked as tired and amped as a junkie as she slid her arm through mine and we began to walk.

The Televisionland I'd been made privy to seemed an illogical place for a gal like Maxine. The kids scattered between sound stages and trailers were mostly jean-clad technician types making busy over walkie-talkies. Peppered among them was an assortment of models dripping with shoulder pads, sequins, and cologne.

Everyone who passed us waved or yelled hello but her eye stayed on me.

"Miss Page, dear, there's so much I wish I could've told you but I have to prepare for tonight's show. Promise me you'll watch Kevin's show tonight, won't you? It's important."

"Don't tell me we can't do this again. I really do want to try and write this book."

"I hope you mean that, Miss Page."

People were parting like the Red Sea to cut a path for her.

"Look, Miss Montego, there's something I should tell you."

She took a step away from me and repositioned the case that had been under her arm since we were midway down the midway.

"Yes, there's something I should tell you, as well."

"Yes?"

Something made her reconsider. "It doesn't matter. God, I should've written a book myself years ago. Why do we always think we have plenty of time? It's funny, about a week ago I started to put together some mementos. To collect as much as I could that spoke to what, if anything, I had accomplished in all my years. It doesn't amount to much, just a single suitcase full of charms. I wish I could give you that suitcase, for posterity."

"Okay. Okay, give it to me and I'll keep it safe for you. When can I get it?"

We stopped in front of a trailer. She took my chin in her hand, demanding my full attention.

"Miss Page, I want you to listen to me very carefully. If you want to write this book badly enough, you will, with or without me. We both know that. But if you don't do your job well, people are going to remember me for things that aren't terribly important. Things I'd rather not be remembered for."

A man in white palazzo pants was waiting at the top of the stairs with a cigarette holder in one hand and a tube of Max Factor in the other.

"Maxine! My favorite queen! Hurry honey, I already poured your coffee."

"I lost my muse, Miss Page. I ignored her so long, she just split and she never came back. Maybe you understand how that works better than some other writer I might've picked up off the boulevard."

"Yeah, I understand it."

Compassion made its way to her face for the first time. "Shame on us."

"Yes, ma'am."

"Inspiration is a flame to be fanned and fueled." An interesting analogy coming from her. "Do whatever you have to do to stay inspired, sweetheart. Life's a little empty otherwise. And remember, Miss Page," she continued while carefully mounting the first metal step, "burning is easy, it's healing that's a bitch."

Ready or not, she was disappearing in front of me.

"Miss Montego, we're not finished."

She continued her ascent.

Maybe I couldn't keep whatever was about to happen from happening but I couldn't let her leave without telling her.

"Ma'am, I know. I know everything."

From the top of the stairs she whispered, "What a burden that must be," as the trailer door slammed closed.

14

❖❖❖❖❖❖

I stood frozen at the foot of her trailer. She was right inside. All that stood between us was aluminum siding. Before deciding my next move, a security guard approached repositioning the walkie-talkie on his belt.

"Miss Page, can I help direct you out of this maze? I know it's a little confusing."

The front gate was checking up on me.

"I think I can find it on my own, thanks."

"Well, actually, Miss Montego thought you could probably use an escort. Just follow me, Miss Page."

He hopped on a motorcycle and rolled forward as I walked back to the car. He waited for me to start the engine and then guided me back to the gate. So she and I were really done talking. I'd been dismissed, very nicely, but dismissed nonetheless.

Why solicit my attention and then push me away? What was the game I'd just been asked to ante up for? Maybe she didn't want me to clear away the doom surrounding her. Maybe I was supposed to observe it, to journal it in her absence.

It was a little after six when I turned back onto the unfamiliar side street that led me to the studio minutes before. Next thing I know, I'm turning into a Sears parking lot and digging in my wallet for Felix's Master Card, which I kept for emergencies. Right then, buying a television was my emergency.

With TV in tow, I pulled into our driveway no more than an hour later than I usually did on a workday.

The television box was much bigger than the television itself and cumbersome as hell. I threw my valise on top of the box and waddled up to the porch, hitting the doorbell with one corner.

When Felix answered the door he met me with a look of controlled amazement. I had to ask him to take the box out of my hands so I could get inside. He was, once motivated, quick to accommodate. When the box was on the coffee table and we were face to face, I realized he had put a curler in his goatee as I had only playfully suggested. It was either to make me laugh or improve his "look." Always hard to tell with him.

I didn't mention it, or touch it, as I hurriedly kissed him, grabbed the scissors, and began stabbing at the seemingly impenetrable cardboard sealed with industrial staples.

"Felix, you forgot to turn the answering machine on again."

That snapped him to attention.

"Oh, no." He ran over and pushed the power button on. "No! I've been in and out of here, like, a million times today, and each time I walk through the door I'm looking at the machine to see if this guy called me."

I'd made my way inside the box but was still unable to rip it open. "Like I say, you should see a light that just stays on in addition to the one that blinks."

"Aaaghghgh!"

"You know, dad, this isn't new technology we're talking about."

"And then, I'm like, oh no, I'm not going to call him. It's his gig. He can just call me. So I waltz out again and, shit! That's, like, a thousand dollar mistake. You think I should call him?"

"How is it you can make the cover of Musician and Down Beat in the same week but you can't harness the power of the answering machine?"

"Maybe I should call him."

"Maybe you should."

"Yeah? Nah, I'm not going to call him now. Jeez, I'll look like a nut. What do you think, Jules?"

Ignoring the argument he was losing with himself, I finally got the box open. Looked like Norman Bates did it but the television was in sight. Before attempting to get it out of its tomb, I grabbed a piece of pizza from an open pizza box in front of me, taking only a couple bites before resuming my project.

Felix automatically began to help me get the television up, out, and plugged it, but he was testy the whole while.

"What the hell were you thinking? I thought we understood each other on this topic. Television is going to bring about the end of the civilized world. Where did you get this, Julie? And what do these things cost, anyway?"

"Hand me that thingy. Thanks."

"This is why you were an hour late? Why didn't you talk to me about this? This is so wrong. We're going to sit here and mold. We're going to get big sores on our asses from sitting in the same place all day."

I wiped Styrofoam and packing dust off my pants and turned on the set. Felix and I took one turn each adjusting the rabbit ears. I flipped stations until I found the Home Shopping Network. We scooted back on the couch eating pizza and refocused our attention to the small beast in front of us.

"Okay, this is going to have something to do with Maxine, right?"

As he spoke, the curler dangling from his chin bobbed around like a dancing marionette. "Just tell me. Does it? Does our new television have anything to do with Maxine?"

"Yes."

"Man, I had this whole fantasy going where you'd come home and none of this shit would be happening."

Right then, a commercial came up with a voice-over that went something like this. "This is a late breaking HSN bulletin. Stay tuned following Maxine Montego's Lap o' Luxury Gemstone Gallery for another visit with the give-away queen herself, Maxine Montego! That's right! She'll be popping in on her good friend, Kevin Quinlin, during his show sometime after midnight for a very special give-away spectacular. She won't give away what she plans to give away. So, let's find out together – tonight on HSN!"

Felix had a mouth full of dough but ceased chewing. I continued to eat but it took some effort.

It was all so odd, hearing her name come over the airwaves. In a way, she seemed like nothing more real than a private thought. But the television was validating her precarious existence for the entire world to hear. I felt marginally violated, like I'd had a dream and somehow it was being broadcast coast-to-coast.

While the announcer spoke, they put up a photograph of beautiful diamond-like jewels shimmering from amidst and beyond the bubbles in a champagne flute worthy of Noel Coward. These baubles were also draped over a magnum-sized bottle of the stuff and scattered across a crisp white linen tablecloth surrounded by folds of blue velvet. In the upper left-hand corner, stylishly scrolled in petal-pink script, was written Lap O' Luxury ~ with Maxine Montego.

"What is really going on here? Maxine has a show? No, I'm hooked up. I would have heard about it."

"It's not music. She sells jewelry."

"Why would she sell jewelry? Why would anybody want her to sell jewelry? What is that guy sticking up his butt?"

He referred to the screen where an exercise segment featuring a perky hostess named Tammy Duke and some weight lifting guru were exploring a device called Fanny-Flex.

The position this device put them in was painful even to watch, yet they were both smiling. I suppose they were smiling with the confidence that their butts were getting smaller each time a disc was fired from their increasingly agile derrieres. According to the guy, Fanny-Flex was a revolutionary product, both doctor tested and dishwasher safe.

We watched, awestruck and dumbfounded. Besides, I wasn't in a hurry to tell Felix the story I had to tell him. Partly because he would hate it and partly because this television show was the most fascinating thing I'd ever seen.

People were calling in and talking about how well the Fanny-Flex worked for them. It's not nice to suggest that people you won't ever know are liars but I had serious doubts that these callers could work something as demanding as the Fanny-Flex. That's all I'm saying.

I certainly couldn't maneuver it. I mean, even if I could get the thing in place, and even if I eventually figured out how to fire it (with those as-of-yet undiscovered muscles), I just know I would never be able to land those tiny discs in that shallow, plastic bull's-eye-painted bowl designed to catch them.

I tried to envision this average caller based on the content of her collective call and the quality of her collective voice. I envisioned a big gal, a Kent menthol in one hand, a box of Little Debbie peanut butter bars in the other. Maybe she's wearing a floral print muumuu slightly perfumed with a little urine from some favorite small dog, and she's watching the set comfortably propped up in an iron lung. But I don't know.

"What is Maxine doing on this show?"

I was too disoriented to give him much of an answer. "Who knows?"

"Even money says you do, Nancy Drew."

I tried to fill him in. He tried to ask appropriate questions. We both tried but were primarily swept up in the warped slice of Americana that is the Home Shopping Network.

A sneak peek at the items coming up in the next hour included the follicle inhibiting Freezer-Tweezer, Sit n' Stay at-home dog training videos and Salad-Go-Round salad shooter. We were forewarned that the salad shooter was only available in limited quantities.

As mesmerizing as it all was, I needed to concentrate. Felix deserved a much better storyteller. So far, he was having a hard time following the plot. And even though he wasn't crazy about what I was sharing, he wasn't livid, either.

"You got in the car with her?"

"No. She got in my car."

"She got in your car? Maxine Montego did?"

"She knows you."

"Knows me? No."

"Yeah. Liner notes. She thinks you're way down, Brown."

"Oh, man. That's why she got in your car?"

"No. She wants me to write a book about her."

"Baby, no offense, but that doesn't make sense."

"No, it doesn't. I think she thinks something bad is going to happen tonight. Like she's about to go to jail or get killed."

"She's heard me play?'

"Are you listening to me at all?"

"But how does she know anything about your writing? Maybe she's trying to get to me through you."

I shot him a dirty look. "Yeah, that makes a lot more sense."

We both turned back to the screen when Maxine's name came up again. This time, it was the perky hostess talking.

"So, word has it that Maxine Montego is going to surprise us all with a special give-away tonight sometime after midnight. What could it be? That Maxine is really something, isn't she?"

The hostess directed only some of the words to the camera. The rest of the time she was talking in brittle tones to someone off camera.

"That's Maxine. You can never call it with her. We just found out she's doing this thing a few minutes ago. No, literally, maybe thirty minutes ago. Nobody knew she was going on Kevin's show, including Kevin. Now we're making announcements every fifteen minutes like a Space Shuttle is about to land or something. Big splashy plans. I just love her to death. Anyway, whatever it is, it'll be so special because she's so special. Really, she's the best. I wouldn't kid around if we weren't close."

Felix articulated what was on my mind: "This chick needs something like maybe Anger-Be-Gone or a Chill-O-Matic."

When the show began a segment on double-knit, polyester ensembles with sequined butterflies appliquéd to the shoulders, I finished explaining. Felix added some thoughtful observations.

"Julie, just call the police. I mean, I thought Maxine Montego was dead until a few days ago. Man, she's one of my heroes. I know I've said some things, but, wow, I'm thrilled she's not dead. Locked up is way better than dead. Odds are she hasn't killed anybody herself. Maybe they'll go easy on her."

"You think?"

"And baby, don't get pissed, but you don't look so good."

"This from a man with a yellow curler pinned to his face." I slid a little closer to his warm sweater and put my head in his armpit, which he pretended to take as an invitation.

"Now you're coming on to me. You want to lick it, don't you? You want to lick this crazy curler, don't you? Just grab it between your teeth and rghrghrghrgh. I know how you are, Spider Girl."

Every time his lips touched my hair, the curler bonked me gently on the forehead. His long arm wrapped around me as he spoke. I burrowed further into the comforting smells of Old Spice and tobacco.

"How long has it been since you slept, Sherlock?"

I fell asleep before answering, my man being the only acceptable pillow at the time. But Felix nudged me back to consciousness when it was announced that Maxine's show was coming up.

I asked Felix to hand me the phone from the end table closest to him. While I had the courage and inclination to do so, I called the cops and explained to the officer that I'd been to the liquor store right before the shootings took place.

"Are you saying you saw the shooting, miss?"

"No. I wasn't there at the time."

"Excuse me?"

"But I saw the man who nodded to the gunmen right before it happened. I was at the liquor store when Maxine got the cigar box the night before."

"I'm sorry. You'll have to slow down, miss. Maxine..."

"Montego."

"Maxine Montego from the television?"

Everybody knew her but me. "Yeah."

"Maxine Montego bought a box of cigars, and you saw it happen."

"Technically, she took them. And I didn't see it. I was out front. But I did untape the clerk after."

"You untaped him? Why did he have tape on him?"

"The cigars were for somebody else. They taped him up so they could take the cigars themselves.

"Who are they?"

"Maxine and her piano player."

"Her piano player."

"No. Listen, something is going to happen tonight if you don't stop it from happening. Something bad."

"Are you being threatened?"

"Not me, Maxine."

There was a brief pause and a nearly inaudible click that made me think we weren't having a private conversation any longer.

"Oh, she's a friend of yours, is she?"

"Well, no, but she wants me to write a book about her."

"Mhmm. Can you see the lady from where you are now?"

"Look, I'm not stalking her. I'm trying to save her."

"Save her, miss? I'm sorry, I didn't catch your name."

I hung up. Felix looked sympathetic as he fingered invisible saxophone keys over the arm of our green frieze couch.

"So you finally call the cops and they give you the cold shoulder."

"I didn't want to call them anyway. Now, what?"

He handed me another slice as Maxine gave us the answer herself.

"Welcome to the Lap o' Luxury! I'm your host, Maxine Montego, and for the next three hours we'll see garnet pendants, jade bracelets, sapphire earrings, I think I heard we even have an opal tiara coming up. So go check your opal tiara and see if it's time for a new one. And, I might even throw in a give-away prior to visiting Kevin, just to keep the show SRO."

Felix stared at the screen wide-eyed and motionless. I couldn't believe I was looking at her there on this little thirteen-inch screen, either. My boyfriend collected himself.

"She looks great. There aren't even any scars. How can she not have any scars? Or wrinkles? I can't believe I'm seeing her. Man, this is intense. What is she doing on there?"

I understood him being a little freaked out.

"You okay, honey?"

"Sure," he snapped, a little too loudly for me to be convinced.

Truth was, she did look beautiful, not at all waxy or lop-eyed, not overly made up in the least. The camera was very kind to her.

"Let's get things started by showing you some of the loot we have coming up. Look at this amazing twelve-carat Brazilian amethyst ring set in beautiful baroque fourteen carat gold. This is item number 772. Fancy cut. And, dig the price. $192.50. That's a preview price, ladies, coming up in just minutes. If you love show stoppers, you'll love that one."

She looked like she had a bad earache, touching the side of her head, brow furrowed, head cocked. After shaking her head at the ceiling, she continued.

"Fourteen carat with genuine sapphire, ruby, and emerald. Your choice for only $11! Don't miss out on, on, on those. And here, look at this, uh, ring. I... I want to give you an idea of the dimensions of this next ring. This is not small. Item number 358. A phenomenal cat's claw bracelet. Just fantastic, isn't it? This comes to you in shivver, shilver..."

She couldn't get it out of her mouth but her frustration was no match for her professionalism.

"Lord, silver plate, that's s-i-l-v-e-r-and is now available in small, medium, large and... It's available in large and extra large."

Small, medium and large? A bracelet? Her eyes wandering off into the distance, and though this was some kind of regular bally she kept spitting, nothing made sense.

It almost seemed that she slid in and out of consciousness at times. One moment, her head would fall back and her mouth would open like she was taking God's communion. The next minute, some imaginary engineer in her head would shout "Rolling" and she'd become alert and eloquent.

She took a phone call but the woman on the other end was more concerned about Maxine's present condition than about ordering jewelry. The hostess got off the phone quickly, explaining that the only thing wrong with her was a virus that was muddling her a little. I used to catch that same virus. I know how sick it can make you.

"How fucked up is she?" Felix asked in hushed reverence.

"She'd have to be pretty loaded by now. She's been popping pills all day.

Listen, her tongue was plenty sharp while I was with her."

He looked at me, then at the screen.

"Jeez, Jules, I wish we could help her."

"I know."

"Looks like she's already mastered the session."

He actually reached out and touched the screen. A very schmaltzy gesture but he did it with great sincerity.

When the phone rang, we both jumped. Felix answered it.

"Yeah? Hey now. Good to hear from you, man. Oh, really? Yeah, we had a little trouble with the answering machine. Yeah. No, I'm still in. Okay. Yeah. Got it."

"That the thousand dollar mistake?"

"Yeah."

"Are you going?"

"I don't know. You good? Come with me, Jules. Maybe I should call him back and give him Benny's number, or tell him I'll lay it down later. What do you think? Should I call him back?"

"Oh, brother, here we go. Go record something. Make some money.

Nothing to be done here anyway, right?"

I undid the bobby pin from the curler. His goat was one big corkscrew curl. It was fun to play with.

"You want to touch it?"

"I am touching it."

"Not that."

"Mmm. Later, gator."

As he picked up the horn case, his voice modulated down a full step. "Will you be here when I get back?" he asked, prepared for the truth this time.

"I don't know," I answered, truthfully.

Felix continued to look at the case in his hand but never came up with anything more to say. When he finished putting on his coat, he turned and looked at me. He was trying to convey his usual nonchalance, but his dark eyes gave him away.

By the time I finished the pizza, Maxine was a stumbling mess but her resilience was impressive. At one point, someone off camera asked if she was going to make it as an arm came into view and the camera wavered a little. Perhaps the cameraman was trying to inconspicuously help balance her before she slid off her pink satin chair. You could tell they were trying to get her off the set but she held her ground. And from that moment on, she never slurred another word, never went cross-eyed, nothing.

"Well, I think it's time to get into some pre-give-away give-aways. Are we ready for that? Why not! I heard the ever charming and always professional Tammy Duke telling you that I'll be popping by Kevin Q's show, maybe in his second hour, to bring you something truly extraordinary. But right now, let's wet your whistles with this."

She had a black velvet board facing her. From it, she pulled out one piece of jewelry at a time, laying them flat or holding them in her elegant, battered hands.

"Here's how it goes. I've only done this a couple of other times and tonight is one of those special occasions when I'm in a housecleaning mood. I'm going to show you pieces from my private collection and if you're the first caller through, I'll personally take down your address while Annette models the goods and you'll get your give-away right away."

The model smiled and nodded.

"Keep in mind these are pieces from my own jewelry box, each one carrying with it a great deal of meaning to me. There's a story attached to each of these little treasures, stories I'm happy to share. So, shall we dance?"

As Maxine painted touching scenarios describing what role each piece played in her glamorous history, people called in. When it was time for an address to be given, Maxine pushed a button on the console to her left and took down the information via an almost unnoticeable earpiece nestled beneath her oxblood curls. You could tell that every caller was in love with her. Though the jewelry was being given for free, I'm convinced that these ladies would've paid through the nose just for a chance to talk to the give-away queen, let alone own a bit of her past.

So I watched her hawk her jewelry and I listened to her recall the last time she'd worn each piece. Sweeping, romantic stories about lost loves and wartime wagers. It was all very moving. She had a way with a story, vivid and intimate.

Though she had remained extremely lucid throughout the give-away portion of the show, management had clearly decided she needed a lie-down and that another host would finish her show that night. Apparently, Maxine only got to stay on while they fished around for a replacement. So, after a station identification, the camera came up on Maxine and Kevin Quinlin. They explained together that because she was 'under the weather' he'd cover for her so she could rest a while. Kevin looked concerned.

She ended by telling her viewers how much they

meant to her and then made them promise to stay tuned.

Over the next fifteen minutes or so I sat staring at the screen, thinking. Kevin added background noise while the Rubik's Cube continued to reposition itself in my head.

I remembered a book on suicide I'd read years ago when the subject was relevant to me. It said that people commonly give away their personal possessions before killing themselves. Is that what was going on here? Was she putting things in order? Perhaps she was preparing for prison. But something else kept gnawing at me. Something was missing. Why didn't anything quite add up? Then the last puzzle piece tumbled into place.

She never mentioned music, never once in any of the stories she told. Never mentioned any of the recording sessions or swank nightclubs those rhinestones must've actually been seen in. Never mentioned anything about the past she'd shared so freely with me earlier that evening.

It figured that the stories she'd told were a bunch of baloney, just sideshow barking, and her lies were as deceptively smooth as the surface of her savagely scarred face.

When the truth started to hit me, it hit me like a spray of machine gun bullets that kept hitting me until I went all the way down. That wasn't her jewelry at all. Those were the smuggled diamonds she was moving. That's what made her such an attractive candidate to those thugs. Who would suspect her? She was known for giving stuff away and it was all so public. Maxine Montego provided a brilliant, audacious solution to a sticky situation.

But how, when the calls were random, could she get the diamonds to the right people? There must've been a trick to it, one I didn't get. The other thing I didn't get was why she was moving them now. She wasn't supposed to do anything until the heat was off. And the heat was definitely not off. The double murder on the corner of 5th and Vanguard was still the top story of the day.

What if she'd decided to take care of things herself? After all, this was Maxine's show and she was plenty pissed about the way everything had come down over the last few days. What if she was angry enough to throw those diamonds away over the tube for all the world, including Thailand, to see? That would definitely make the ultimate give-away, the last of the Montego Supremes. Of course, if she was dumping real diamonds on women who would never know they were real, if she had those big fat jewels set in cheap 10K gold and silver-plated tin, she was going to be in trouble, tumor-sized trouble.

And surely, she knew it. Surely, she knew it when she asked a perfect stranger to drive her around all day, keeping her out of the house, keeping her a moving target. She knew it when she blew off Peter, getting him far enough away so that he couldn't alter her intentions or resolve. She knew it when she went back to her favorite hangout, one last time, and when she told a complete nobody some of her innermost thoughts. She took a chance on me because she truly didn't have time to shop.

And she must have known for a while that she was about to die. Long enough to lead her to collect what she felt substantiated her existence and stash it away in a suitcase for safekeeping. Maybe she wanted me to figure out her little con before she checked out. She knew I'd hunt her down if I unscrambled the puzzle in time. She just wasn't sure I would. But I did.

I didn't wait to hear that there weren't going to be any more give-aways on Kevin Quinlin's show, though I wondered if Peter was waiting patiently at the studio for her thinking she was still inside. If he and the jewel thieves and cops were waiting, as she'd baited them all to do. Yeah, that might provide an extra hour or so of freedom to finish her business as she saw fit.

I got in my car and took off toward the hills. And yes, I was hoping I could stop her but I'd come too far to merely read about this final chapter in tomorrow's paper. I wanted to be there when it all came down. By now, she owed me that.

15

❖❖❖❖❖❖

I sped across town like Speed Racer. Seemed like I'd driven to Maxine's so many times by then, the car needed no additional guidance from me.

As I turned onto 5th Street, a piece of paper flew in through my open window. It flew in and slapped itself against my face, remaining there for a second before landing on the seat beside me.

I dove as far as the steering wheel would allow, snatching it tenuously between frozen fingers. It was a loose page from somebody's notebook. There was nothing on it, a perfectly blank page; the thing that scares me most.

Immortalizing the drive further was a sky making the oddest sound I've ever heard a sky make. It wasn't thunder exactly, more like huge sheets of tinfoil ripping. Muffled, abbreviated little tugs. And it was cold, as cold as it had been for the last three days. Yeah, I could've had the window up but frankly I felt like being cold, kept me alert.

Fortunately, the radio wasn't breaking in with anything that affected me personally. No shoot-outs at the Home Shopping Network. No dead guys in black Cadillacs. So far, so good.

I passed the now-boarded-up Liquor Palace with only a glance, pushing to remain calm as I ran light after light. And for the first time in over five years I found myself waxing nostalgic over the prescription drugs that had previously monopolized my life. The drugs that had strung me up like a piñata for the world to beat the shit out of until my guts were strewn across the West Coast, hard candy for the masses.

I'd wasted my integrity, time, and much of my life on those soul-numbing cough drops and this old woman was somehow coaxing me back down that barbed wire cul-de-sac. Soon I'd be writing again, I was sure of it. I guess I couldn't imagine one without the other. And I saw clearly the girl I thought I'd buried several years ago. It had been a long time since I'd taken a good look at myself but there I was, an addict who'd never stopped searching for a new addiction. The stony logic of my life concluded for me in a flash of acquiescence as cold as that late night drive.

But there was no drug available. So, I filed this revelation and began to brace myself for what I was driving into. If Thailand got there before me and I walked in anyway, that would make me the biggest idiot ever, and the deadest, but there was no reconsidering now.

I turned down the beautiful block that was to be the next crime scene deposited in my memory bank.

A single bulb housed in a gigantic, Spanish-looking lantern illuminated the porch. I started to ring the bell then considered it an empty gesture in that I was going in anyway. Besides, if the thugs were already in there they weren't going to be any nicer to me for having rung first.

There was no doorknob on the great Mediterranean door, only a black, wrought iron bar attached vertically. Eyeing the wooden shutters I'd stood beside the night before, I figured I'd have to somehow crawl through one window or the other. Fortunately, before I tried that, I tried the door. She hadn't locked it.

I entered the foyer to the overwhelming smell of gasoline. My All-Stars slid across black and white marble tiles slick with fuel. Two one-gallon cans were propped against an inside wall. I picked one up. Empty.

There was a small semi-circular table pushed against that same wall. On it was a photograph of a fine looking redhead. The picture was old and the colors weren't terribly true but the yellow boots still looked as vibrant and trendy as I'd imagined.

The photo was taken from the vantage point of the audience. You could see the backs of several heads in what looked like quite a crowd. The singer had a benevolent smile on her open face, one arm pulling the mic stand to the right of her frame, the other extended to an audience member reaching up toward her, as were several others.

As far as the rest of the action on stage, you could only see the drummer who was directly behind her on a small platform. A handsome sonofabitch, all bad news and dirty fun by the looks of him. A graduate of the Gene Krupa school of style.

His left drumstick hung just above a high-hat, his right rested on the rim of a snare. He was flashing a devastating smile and his complete attention was on her or her ass. It was hard to tell.

Obviously things were swinging just about as

hard as things swing. There was something so visceral about the snapshot, I almost wished I'd been there. Then I wondered which of those innocent looking drumsticks took out the singer's eye a moment later.

She had the 3 x 5 displayed in a huge red leather frame. Red and leather, fire and skin. For whatever reason, I took an extra moment to pop it out of the frame and into my coat pocket.

I poked my head in the front room and gave it a cursory once-over. It presented a graceful kind of nonchalance. The kind of room that lets you know each piece is valuable yet invites you to put your feet up anyway.

The formal dining room on the left of the foyer was tailored and vacant, as well. She had planted herself, or was planted, deeper in the house. I would have to move further away from the front door than I cared to.

I thought about calling out her name but was too afraid to do that. It seemed like the longest hall I've ever walked down as I crept by and peered in three rooms before locating my meal ticket.

The master bedroom housed impeccably maintained Danish Modern furniture sporting burgundy bakelite handles and knobs on the vanity, side tables, and highboy. The bed had one of those backboards with the slide-open book compartments built in. Classically thin white chenille covered the bed and two large brass reliefs, one a female Pierrot character, the other male, hung against one wallpapered wall. Lamps, pillows, and pictures, all strikingly in fashion again, as contemporary as they were in the 50s.

This was the first room in the hallway that I actually entered. I could see it was hers and thought she just might be nestled limp and lifeless in the adjacent master bath to the left of the dresser. No. Just a lot of pink and black tile and a tiny set of three plaster fish above the toilet. No slit-wristed junkie filling the tub with remorse. But then, why bother with gasoline if you're going to do it like that? Incidentally, this was the only room she hadn't doused.

Gasoline stained the remaining length of the sleek, stylish house. I followed this death trail to the last room on the left. That door was ajar. Choking back fear and fumes, I carefully pushed it open an inch or two more then stood still waiting for a sound to inform me of my next move. It came in the form of pills scattering.

Throwing the door open wide, I found Maxine in a recliner at the back of a large blue room outlined in gold. The recliner was reclining, though she wasn't using the footrest. Her legs were tucked underneath her, cozy-like. She looked so tiny in the middle of the over-stuffed tweed.

She didn't look as good as she had on television. The waxy build-up was once again apparent and her now evident glass eye had somehow gotten jostled a little to the left. The Second Skin puckered atop the beveled flesh surrounding her good eye. Perhaps she'd cried too much that day even for latex and grease paint. It didn't matter. She wasn't crying now. She was sleeping – with her eyes wide open.

The bottle of whatever she'd been taking all day was on the floor. Water, too. Some tablets were still on the table next to the chair.

A rhinestone lighter just like the one she gave me was in her left hand, barrel aimed up. Ironically, that which had seemed less dangerous once its true purpose was revealed now seemed the most dangerous weapon of all. One pull on the silver plated trigger and everything would go up, including me.

I thought she was looking right at me until I took a few steps in. She wasn't looking at me. She was looking at the door I'd come through, unblinking. When I moved toward her and out of the doorframe, I tripped on a large suitcase placed behind another chair. Surely this was the suitcase she'd told me about, her suitcase of treasures.

My soles squished on a Persian rug bloated with gasoline. Both lungs were working hard and I couldn't help but cough and sputter.

I looked at her for some reaction then glanced at the albums framed along the opposite wall. I wanted to go take a closer look but there were more important observations to make. Was she with it? Was she dead? Was I?

"Mmmis Page. Yes, I can sssee you're writing as we speak."

She started blinking, pulling herself back to consciousness from the trance that held her. Her speech remained labored on and off. Words badly slurred, then not at all. But even when it took her an extra beat to articulate something she was never less than cogent, extraordinarily poised and in control under the circumstances.

"I am exxxpecting company but was hoping you would not be among the guests at this particular soiree. Or perhaps I was hoping you would be, I don't know. I wasn't sure if involving you further would help or harm you but I'm a selfish woman."

"That's funny, Miss Montego. I've been struggling with that same question regarding you."

"Yes, I imagine you have. I thought I saw enough desperation in your young, troubled face to suggest that you just might pop by in time for the festivities. The suitcase behind that chair is yours, if you like. I have enough baggage."

"Thanks. Nice house."

"Isn't it?"

"How did you get home?"

"Cab. Natch. Tell me Miss Page, do you understand what you've walked into?"

"Yes."

"Then you understand that as sssoon as my company arrives, after only a brief exchange of civilities, I'll be setting my house on fire."

"I can see that. Yes."

"Wwwhen I pull this trigger, it will become difficult to get out of here. I've strategized the disbursement of gas to optimize the results."

"I want to stay. I'll take my chances."

"I can appreciate that. I've taken mine. Well, then, I've done my bit. You're on your own. God, I'd like a cigarette." She fingered the cigarette box on the side table then flicked at a pill with one ridiculous nail.

"How many of those have you taken?"

"Thirty."

I was caught between panic and admiration.

"You're so gullible. I'm joking."

"Right."

"I promise you, there's no pill in the world strong enough to do me any real harm. I know because I've tried them all. Today, I've been particularly careful to monitor my consumption. Just enough to keep me centered. Hopefully, I've timed things well."

"Hopefully. Look, Miss Montego, please don't do this. Please don't. It would be such a stupid waste."

"Yes. The world of cubic zirconium will never fully recover from the loss."

I didn't know what to say. All I knew was I didn't want her to kill herself, not on my dime, not in front of me. And I wasn't ready to have my own burnt skin peeled back by some overworked paramedic. I fully intended to walk out of there whole.

There were a lot of questions I wanted answered but they all took a back seat for a moment to the cold hard facts pinching the side of my neck and running down my left leg. The air was unbearably heavy. My headache returned.

I needed to buy some time. I figured that as long as she was talking I could keep her from pulling the trigger, so I'd keep her talking. That was my plan and I'd stick with it until I could figure out a really good one. Of course, somebody was bound to show up in a few minutes but I'd deal with that then.

"So, how did the diamonds get into the country?"

As those words came out of my mouth I could not have cared less how the diamonds came into the country. But the ensuing conversation bought me the time I needed. In fact, it bought me everything I own today.

"Yes. Let's do this. Tape recorder?"

Again with the tape recorder. "I don't have a tape recorder."

She made a feeble attempt to aim my attention

across the room. I didn't get it. Subtle wasn't going to work with the likes of me.

"For Christ's sake. Go get the fucking tape recorder out of that table drawer over there. Do you really think you're going to remember everything? Don't you want evidence? Are you a fucking moron?"

Sometimes I am a fucking moron but that was just nasty. I slowly moved across the room, the whole while keeping an eye on her weapon of choice.

Whatever dream-state had her slurring words only moments prior had vanished, and the venom flowed from her as freely as New Year's Eve champagne. Anger is such an empowering emotion. Throughout the rest of our chat, she never slurred another word or faded off in the middle of a sentence. Her voice, however, was particularly hoarse and only marginally above a whisper.

I located the recorder and checked that it had a cassette inside. It was such a small thing, fit right in my palm.

As I familiarized myself with it, I took some guarded comfort in thinking that she must've thought I'd walk away. Otherwise, a recording wouldn't really be that necessary.

Adjusting my glasses, I checked the volume and positioned myself maybe three feet from her. My hand was shaking, which she noticed but kindly chose to ignore. As I hit record, she shook her head at the ceiling and tried to clear her instrument.

"A Thai shipping company contacted me one lucky night, my new found celebrity having made its way across the continents. They are one of the major exporters of the jewelry and novelties sold on

HSN. And within this company is another clandestine company."

"Only this company exports actual jewels."

"See how good you are? These are stolen jewels, diamonds to be exact, brought in and fenced to a highly select clientele. A very powerful man owns the company, a man I already knew in another context at another time in my life. When he heard what I was doing for a living, he called in a favor."

"Happy Man?"

She tried to smile but when she parted her lips, a slow leak of air came out, audible and unsettling.

"I'm not even going to ask how you know about him. I'll assume it's from the news."

"I was the one crouched outside your window last night, the one you saw pulling away in the Honda."

Wistful admiration flushed her face.

"How resourceful. I thought that might have been you. Tell me, why did you kick the wall?"

"Because I'm no good at this shit."

"That's right. I remember how well you tailed me. Yes, Happy Man."

"He asked you to be his fence."

"You could say he asked. Saying no to him isn't always the smartest thing to do."

"Sounds like saying yes kind of sucks, too."

Again, she tried to smile but the latex was fighting her every step of the way.

"I don't know if he would've made the call if he merely found out I was hosting a television show. But he loved the idea that I'd become famous for giving things away. His method was simple enough. Took some setting up on my end with the studio but they already had me pegged as a trouble-maker and a diva so my request for a private phone line didn't really stick out as all that odd. I could receive the stuff comfortably and, more to the point, give it away over the airwaves to clients posing as customers. I'd take as many calls as I needed to, waiting for one of the callers to use a certain password in our conversation. Those people were "chosen" as my give-aways. Brilliant."

"This stuff looks like jewelry when it gets here?"

"Absolutely. No loose stones. One three inch butterfly hair clip would be shipped in a separate box and the other 50,000 shipped in crates, the box coexisting with the other merchandise."

"Cigar boxes?"

"Isn't that adorable? That came later, my special touch. I thought it would be cute to package the particularly high-dollar diamonds in something distinguished like a cigar box and call them Montego Supremes. The boys on the docks would know to hand deliver those boxes, keep them off the big trucks altogether."

"Wasn't that pretty dangerous considering your celebrity?"

"Unnecessary is the word most commonly associated with it."

"Why would Happy Man let you call a shot like that? Why would he let you put your name on the boxes?"

"At that point, I had him by the jewels, so to speak. To some degree, anyway. It was such an ingenious method of fencing that he was neither ready to stop doing it, nor to get some less established host involved. He hated the idea of Montego Supremes, but I loved it. So plans were made to have the cigar boxes shipped separately as if it was an entire shipment of cigars. Cigars from Thailand. Isn't that a gas?"

This time, she did smile, and when she did, all the edges of her face puckered, the mask begging to be removed. I wondered if the fumes were dissolving her topcoat.

She rubbed her forehead with the butane barrel then readjusted her legs to the other buttock, and I wondered if I'd just missed my only opportunity to nab the lighter. All I could do was watch, impotent and sweaty.

"Why did you want your name on those boxes? Seems more than unnecessary."

"You think I have a death wish? Anyway, these shipments weren't marked for the Home Shopping Network. They were marked for a tobacco company. They would be distributed to a liquor store in the area and then bought by a special customer looking for that special cigar. Moi. I would drop by and pick up a box, no one the wiser. No one except the two cats who drove the van downtown and the gentleman behind the counter."

"Sandy."

She wiping one tired, sagging socket with the butt of her hand. The rubbing movement inadvertently corrected the placement of her glass eye.

"We stopped moving them over the television, which, ingenious though it was, hadn't been the easiest thing, phone lines and operators and all. With this new system, I could distribute them under the guise of strictly street give-aways, premieres, shopping malls, wherever we decided. But the dumb fucks who drove the boxes downtown, well, I'm sure you know all about that. So, it wasn't my name that got anyone killed. It was greed."

"A box of greed with your name on it."

"Touché."

"Why would you say yes to that? You were already famous. You were already rich."

"Not that famous. Not that rich. Look, kid, the furniture I have, I've had for decades. The furniture and the house and the company I keep. And I don't mean to sound depressing or anything, but I've had some notable medical expenses."

"What about the money you make with the television show?"

"It looks like real money but it isn't."

I pursed my lips against a smile I wasn't willing to give her, adjusted my weight from one spongy shoe to the other.

"Jesus, I don't know what makes us do what we do. But here we all are, having done what we've done. Besides, I don't like owing anybody anything and up until last week, I felt I still owed that bastard for helping me out of a jam years ago."

I tried to cough but my attempt to suck in enough air to do so proved to be painful and futile. My throat was being ripped to shreds by the liquid I was standing in. "You all right, Miss Page?"

I continued to choke and sputter. "How can you talk through these fumes?"

She pulled delicately at the bangs of her wig.

"Well, I've been smoking longer than you have."

Collecting myself, I hurriedly continued so as to not lose her attention. "So what changed last week?" Her obvious discomfort with that question had me reaching for the next. "What big favor did this guy do for you?"

She chose her words carefully now, not lying and not yet willing to spill any more than she wanted, editing as she spoke. "He got me my first recording contract in 1954. Well, he bought it, actually."

"Wow. You have known him for quite awhile."

"A lifetime."

"So, because he bought your first contract, you turned to a life of crime? I'm sorry, ma'am but that doesn't make sense. What's missing?"

She had that long distance stare creeping across her face again. Then she slowly picked up another pill and placed it gently on her tongue. I believe she chose to tell me the truth at that point only because she had no tomorrows left to protect.

"That baby you're longing to know about."

"Yes?"

"It was his, a baby boy."

I could see it was hard for her to share it but, God forgive me, I wanted that information. And though I might've been able to hunt it down some other way, it would be most rewarding coming from her.

"Thank you, Miss Montego. Thank you. Tell me what happened?"

"It was 1955 and my career was taking off in a big, splashy way. I couldn't afford to be pregnant. I told him I wanted out, that I didn't want to sing anymore, that I would rather be a mom. He said he didn't believe me. How could I raise a baby on my own? He was married at the time, to the same cunt he's married to now, as it turns out, so he couldn't marry me. He convinced me that the best thing to do would be to have the baby and give him up for adoption. Reluctantly, that's what I did. I turned the gig over to Louis at the Sahara and went into hiding for the better part of eight months. When the baby was born, the Happy Wanderer promised me he would take care of everything and that my baby would be placed in the best possible situation. I tried to move forward after that, and to never look back.

"You didn't have any other children?"

"Couldn't. The 'doctors' he'd provided told me there had been complications during the delivery. My female parts had been removed in an attempt to save my life."

"I think maybe I complain too much," I interjected under my breath.

"So last week, apropos of nothing, I get a call from... Do you hear something?"

I shifted my head but not my feet, attempting to listen for what I didn't want to hear. "No, I don't," I answered as my neck muscles tensed. Her face was peeling back dramatically now giving her an even more unreal quality than usual.

"Hold on to that recorder, darling, our company has arrived."

I could feel my neck muscles contract as the indisputable sound of footsteps approached.

"Hello, Maxine."

A very old Asian man entered. He was shorter than Peter and half his size but boy-howdy, he could dress. A floor-length, black fur coat hung open over a dark grape silk suit, thin lapels, double breasted. The buttons looked like some kind of dark, precious stones. He sported a white lily boutonniere and bleached white alligator shoes. Jeweled earrings hung from both ears and his white Nehru collar divided the darkness of his jacket and face with purpose. Looked like some nouveau cult leader. His cologne pierced the gasoline.

"Maxine, precious. It's been too long."

"Hello, boss. Unescorted this evening?"

"Boss. That's funny coming from you, Maxine. You always call your own shots. We both know that." He stroked his coat as he spoke as if petting a cat. "Yes. I told the boys to wait for me on the ship. I was hoping for a private moment with you."

On that note, he smiled and nodded at me, then discreetly took out a linen handkerchief and coughed into it. Apparently the fumes were unavoidable to everyone but Maxine.

Positioning himself behind the chair that faced Maxine, he tried to push the suitcase aside with one shoe but couldn't manage it. The suitcase wouldn't budge.

"A personal visit from the top brass. I'm flattered. Sit down, won't you?"

"Maxine, I can't stay. I'm sorry that we won't have more time to catch up. I have always cherished our time together so very much."

"How charming. Oh, do forgive me. This is my biographer, Julie Page. Miss Page this is Happy Man. Tell me, don't you feel a little silly being introduced like that?"

He chuckled, smiling warmly. "Maxine, you are so very funny."

His voice was seductive, downright hypnotic, and it was clear that he liked Maxine quite a lot. Even through her clipped retorts, the exposition of their shared past was almost audible between them.

"How do you do, Miss Page. Yes, there you are recording our conversation as we speak. Unfortunately, the fact that you are here puts your future in more than serious question, I'm afraid. Please don't take it personally."

He pulled out a pistol, no rhinestones, from an inside pocket. He didn't do anything too threatening with it. He just held it in his left hand revealing a gold watch so yellow it looked fake, and turned back to Maxine. Then he leaned on the back of the chair, both hands resting on the frame. I fumbled to retrieve the recorder.

Though he wasn't aiming the gun my way, I fully understood that he intended to as soon as he finished his conversation. Burnt or shot, things weren't looking good for me.

"Precious, you know why I'm here."

"You've come to kill me."

"I wouldn't let anyone else near you. Dreadful oafs. My respect for you would not allow that. So, I thought tonight we could see one another one last time. However, as usual, you have decided how things will end. A fire. How perfect, Maxine. And how beautiful you will be within it."

"You say the nicest things."

"What will I ever do to trace the jewels you gave away tonight, my little minx?"

"Hopefully, I've made that very difficult. Only I heard the addresses and I paid an intern, handsomely, to have them couriered before I left the studio. It's awe-inspiring what money can buy, isn't it? Besides, hunting down each housewife the jewels are being delivered to would put way too much attention on you. You don't need any more of that right now, the way I figure it. Are you proud of me? You always said I made you proud."

He contracted his face in an "Ooh, that felt good" sort of way, and smiled."You have created quite a situation for me, my dear. A situation that pushes me to do this thing I do not want to do. Sweetheart, in this final moment, may I ask why?"

"Didn't you hear the news today, boss?"

Mild concern replaced ambivalence. "I am afraid I did not."

"The cops found a motorcycle, a Harley-Davidson motorcycle, at the bottom of the wash behind the power plant, a motorcycle registered to Sander Harper."

"I see. You betrayed me over the clerk. Yes, I asked my people to take care of that. He was a, what is the expression, a loose cannon, Maxine. Surely you understand that, dear."

"No one was supposed to get hurt – dear."

"I apologize."

"You apologize? I have blood on my hands because of you. We had a deal. No one gets hurt. But then, I now understand that there has never been any honor in your word. You know, I've made deals with you and deals with the devil and I've got to say I prefer the devil."

I thought I heard her voice crack with emotion but it was so scratchy and hushed, I couldn't be sure.

"What are you talking about, Maxine?"

"Oh, didn't you know? I got a call from the little woman last week."

"What little woman?"

"Your cunt wife, Happy. That was a shocker! I only met her once, the night I met you, fifty years ago.

Out of some twisted sense of priority, she thought I should know about my son."

I was lost but he seemed to know exactly what was coming.

"No."

"Yes. She knew all about our little affair a century ago. Claims you told her at the time. In that she couldn't give you an heir herself, you two were the lucky kids who raised my baby. How convenient. Almost like you planned it that way. Thanks for placing him in such a safe, nurturing environment."

"Maxine, let me explain."

"I don't think I can take in any more information right now. Thanks anyway. I understand he grew to be quite a powerful man in your organization, and that he died honorably. That sure put my mind at ease, to know he died honorably, protecting your business interests. Oh, yes, and that his funeral...his funeral was lovely. So now I know how he lived, and how he died. As a mobster. Wasn't that decent of her?"

"She is an old woman, Maxine. It is a fresh wound for her. She is mourning him, as am I. He was her only son, a smart businessman, an asset from the beginning. Maxine, we both loved him very much. She shouldn't have called you but..."

"Oh, hey, if there's anything I can do to ease her pain."

"And, of course, this is why you betrayed me tonight."

"No. No, it isn't," she practically barked. "I allowed my son to be taken away from me. I take full responsibility for ruining his life. Sandy, on the other hand, wasn't my fault, goddamnit. How could you?"

You could see his wheels spinning, searching for some disarming retort. "Don't the things we've accomplished together outweigh the indiscretions?"

She ceremoniously pointed the lighter at Diamond Jim.

"Hardly," she hissed. And with that, pulled the trigger.

17
❖❖❖❖❖❖

When the sound stopped reverberating in my ears and my vision came flooding back through the shock of horror that had blinded me momentarily, I began to comprehend what happened.

He still stood at the back of the easy chair clutching the headrest with one hand, his unnecessary pistol with the other. Lips slightly parted, his expression was one of frozen nonchalance. Very much the expression you see on a wax figure in a museum.

There was one tiny hole above his brow. A clean hole. No blood. The back of his head, however, was gone. Globs of red-brown gravy collected at the top of his fur collar then rolled down. Bits of brain sprayed out covering the back wall like a child's spin art at a school carnival.

The bile that came out of me came quickly and without warning. One hard wave of nausea, one hard belch of fluid, thankfully missing the recorder that had fallen to the floor.

Too stunned to scream or run or speak, I simply remained bent staring at my vomit as a focal point through the fear that bathed both lenses.

Wiping them dry, I picked up the recorder, which

was amazingly still running. I figured if I had the tape, my chance of survival was greatly increased. She wanted the tape to make it out of there.

When I straightened up, Maxine was leaning the shiny hot barrel against her temple, stroking her thumb along the rhinestone handle.

"I had it designed to look exactly like a lighter," she quipped.

My knees buckled and then locked. The snot framing my upper lip mixed with the salt-water tears that dripped into my gaping hole. I thought of my dog, Bullet, a dog I'd had when I was a kid.

"My God, that was a freak bit of luck, wasn't it? A very lucky shot. Of course, I wasn't aiming for his head."

Trying to be present yet innocuous, I kept my gaze averted from both her and him.

"He doesn't look all that happy to me," she observed, then produced a Bic lighter from under the cushion while seriously considering my current state.

"Are you in there, Miss Page?"

"Yes." I could hardly hear myself respond.

"I liked Sandy. No one was supposed to get hurt."

"Okay."

"Are you all right? God fuck it, I asked you if you knew what you were walking into."

"I'm sorry."

She placed her feet square on the footrest of the recliner, elbows on knees, one supporting a gun, one supporting a lighter.

"Don't give it a thought. What's a little vomit with all this gas and blood. It's just a carpet. Besides, I'm the one who's sorry," she said, exhaling slowly. "In that the recorder is still recording and you're not, I'm going to wrap things up. For the record, I hope you make it out of here. This time, I'm going to make sure I don't. I'll be chasing the fire with a bullet in a moment, as I need to be sure."

When she brought her feet up closer to her butt, it forced her elbows down between her thighs. Her knees were at her shoulders and she looked like a human grasshopper, an origami sphinx. Both weapons were pointing straight into the room.

"It's unfortunate that this is the thing that will put me back on the charts. This is not what my life has been about."

My hand was shaking like a gal whose life had never been in danger before. She began to rock back and forth as I'd seen her do in the car and her eyes kept darting around the room, vacant and lost. But I could see that on some level, she was excited by the poetic implications of the cruel, selfish act in front of her.

After all, she was about to inflict on an unsuspecting television audience the suicide of the hour. She was about to break an unbreakable contract with Bangkok's premier bogeyman by taking both protagonist and antagonist out of the picture. And she would face no trial. And she would face no pity.

She called it, no one else. She orchestrated it. And as an added perk, she would get to revisit, if only for a moment, that night a few decades ago when she saw the white heat of her life's passion burn from the inside out. She stood that close to it. She got to see how fire really works. I'm pretty sure nothing else came close to that experience for her. And now she would burn again.

She began muttering, "Someone needs to write a book about what it actually means to be an artist. Not this current wave of bullshit preaching journal writing and mantras and how to get in touch with your creative inner child for Christ's sake. There should be one illuminating book that lays out the horrors and the price you'd better be willing to cough up and how to reassess what the fuck success really is. Something that would scare away those too weak to handle it and maybe encourage the rest. Could you do that? And remember to at least mention my music, would you? Love the art, not the artist."

She smiled apologetically.

"I'll immortalize your music. Felix could have you back on the radio with two phone calls."

"Immortalize my music! You really have a flair for the dramatic, Page."

"I'm dramatic?"

"My music immortalized. That's sweet, kid. Maybe you really could get Felix Mint to run with some of it."

"We can do a lot of things, but not this. Don't do this. Don't do it to Peter."

"Peter. Yes. Where is Peter? Well, he'll probably come by later on, once everything has been hosed down. That's best anyway. He doesn't deserve to die like this. He hasn't earned it."

"Don't."

"Yeah, why not you? You take the music. I, Maxine Montego, give you, Julie Page, full ownership of my musical library. All copyrights and licensing are to be turned over to you as of today. Oh, that's rich. Priceless," she laughed.

Out of nowhere, the body that had remained standing changed its mind. The corpse collapsed in a pile of damp fur. He fell backwards and on his side so as to face me. The fall jarred his jaw some and his eyes had rolled up a degree.

After a beat or two of staring at this midnight matinee swamp creature, I screamed. I screamed in a way I was unaware I could. A Jamie Lee Curtis kind of scream almost more frightening than my company.

"Okay." Maxine cleared her throat. "That must be my cue. I'm on."

"No, please. Don't do this. Please don't do this."

Then she began to sing. "...as a rule, fate is never less than cruel. And I'm nobody's fool."

"I'm begging you, Maxine."

"I know what you're thinking." She put the gun down, picked up a cigarette, and lit it.

"Oh, God, no."

"You're thinking I smoke too much."

With one good deep drag behind her, she threw the cigarette onto the rug and the party began.

Fire raced around the room blazing patterns she'd stenciled earlier. Around the floorboards. Around certain pieces of furniture. Her chair was untouched. She must've wanted to watch it all for as long as possible. She lit another cigarette and picked up the gun, curling herself like a cat on the cushion, staring, wide-eyed and dreamy as the curtain went up behind her.

The fire had exited the room by the time my stomach uncramped and I started thinking clearly enough to act. The fire got noisy fast and I had to raise my voice for her to hear me. "Give me the gun."

I put the recorder in the jacket pocket that hid the photo and stepped toward her, right up to the footrest. She aimed the gun at my face. I moved away on instinct then decided she didn't mean it, reaching out my hand with a steadiness that had not been mine until then. "Give me the gun."

She pulled back the hammer.

"Fuck you!" I yelled, bravely.

"Why don't you run, you little fool." Her strained voice growled aggressively over the din.

"Fuck you!" I yelled again, this time, crying openly. "Don't do this. Don't make me leave you in here. Fuck you! I won't do it."

Her face grew somber and still, like sleep.

"Julie, look at it. Isn't it thrilling? Just step toward the hall and look for a moment."

I did. Not because I needed a thrill right then, but because it occurred to me that my exit space was probably getting smaller. It was. Much smaller. And she was right, it was majestic. Like a million candles lining the hall, growing bigger and more powerful as I watched.

Flames danced along my left cuff. Blood bubbled across black knuckles where skin had been while I frantically tried to pat out the smoldering wool sleeve.

I turned again to my artistic albatross as she continued singing to no one. I could hear her one-in-a-million voice cutting through the smoke like a foghorn. "... and I'm nobody's fool." Then she put the barrel of the shimmering gun in her shimmering mouth, and pulled the trigger one last time.

Again I screamed, but this time all emotion was lost over a wall of crackling heat and snapping flames.

I realize now it was a nice thing she did for me, knowing I couldn't leave without her. I'm sure she would've preferred to watch a little longer if I hadn't been such a wet blanket.

Mute, I began to make my way down the hall. I couldn't run. The flames were wildly cheering me on yet remained close to each wall. Like a dignitary walking through a semi-controlled, overly zealous crowd, I proceeded cautiously. And I made it all the way to the front door relatively unscathed. The fire had created some weird air pressure situation that made it hard to get the big door open but I managed it then threw myself on the lawn, putting into practice what we hope we'll never have to. I was rolling and gasping and yelling "help" and "oh, God," but the lawns are awfully far apart in that neighborhood.

Once on my feet I began to run, aiming for a neighbor's house. Then it occurred to me that the suitcase was inside. The only clues as to who she used to be were stranded in a burning building. When that was gone, it was gone. All those irreplaceable treasures and charms. All that information.

I've been called a lot of things in my life, stupid is certainly one of them. But running back in wasn't stupid, despite public opinion, despite the scars. Running back in was the smartest thing I've ever done.

Stepping through fire to get past the doorframe, I ran down the hall this time, flames glomming onto me like locusts. I pitifully swatted at my arm and the back of my head, running sideways as if I would burn less that way. But I kept my right hand in my pocket the whole time, shielding a recorder and a photograph, and a roll of Tums I'd forgotten was in there.

Happy Man was where I'd left him, though I didn't remember that the suitcase was between his corpse and the chair he had been clutching. Now, I remembered.

There was very little wall left untouched by the fire at that point but everything toward the center of the room was still intact. The fur coat was smoldering but the chair wasn't. I threw myself against the headrest, rolling against it, a lone life preserver in a sea of flames.

Grabbing the suitcase, I looked up to see Maxine one last time. Her chair was beginning to burn. As yet, she was not. The way her face was positioned, head tilted back, mouth wide open, it looked like she was still singing.

The journey back out of hell's house was quick but destructive and the suitcase, heavier than imagined. I ran, trying to ignore the flames covering my clothes and hair. Each lick stung and stabbed at my nerve endings but the fact that I couldn't breathe was what kept me flying.

I continued to burn and scream and drag that suitcase with my free left hand all the way to the grass. Seemed so far away. If anyone had been watching from a nearby window it would've made a memorable scene, me running across that huge lawn, burning, dragging a suitcase.

I had extinguished myself before making it to the car, but really, any amount of time you're on fire is too long.

My knees gave out before the car key hit its mark.

Shrieks of pain escaped when I went down. The very impact of the grass on my wounds was almost more than I could bear.

I stroked my stinging scalp and came back with a handful of my own hair, black and mangled.

Sheer will got the suitcase in the back seat because I can't imagine now how I ever managed it as breathless and burnt as I was. With the car door standing open, I tried again for a neighbor's house, staggering onto a porch, ringing the bell, and choking out with what little voice I had left, "Fire! Fire! Help!" After what seemed like an interminable amount of time, the porch light went out. An icy response, don't you think? I could only hope they went to call the cops.

In that I didn't have time to beg everyone on the block, I decided to drive down the hill myself and get help. By the time I got back to the car my adrenaline rush had drastically subsided. I wasn't moving very well. My arms could barely be raised to grip the car door as I coughed out more bile and smoke.

It was while balancing myself between the frame of the car and my car door that the Cadillac came skidding around the corner. It made such a whoosh as it passed me that my chest tightened, anticipating yet another catastrophe.

Peter lurched the black beauty to a sloppy conclusion barely entering the driveway. The door flew open and he flew out, one gesture, not two. Light flickered through the closed blinds and I could clearly imagine how bad things had gotten in there.

He ran to the porch yelling, "Max! Max! Jesus, please, no."

I wanted to call out but really, why? What good

would that do him now? Anyway, this was a private moment. I didn't belong in it.

He held himself at the door then backed up a couple of steps, looking for some other means of entering. Then back to the doorframe, all the while yelling his grief at each sadistic flame. Finally, he sat on the porch stoop, put his head in his hands and sobbed.

It was the saddest thing I hope I ever have to see. This piano player seemed to always be bringing up the rear when it came to Maxine, covering for her, tending to her, bowing down when better judgment did not prevail. I disliked her in that moment seeing what she had left him to deal with. Despite a shared circumstance, they were fundamentally very different people. It wasn't his fault that he couldn't bring himself to run into burning buildings.

It did cross my mind that if he had, just that once, if he had run in and dragged out her charred remains, even if he'd tried to, his inadequacy would no longer be the thing that defined him, to him. He could've lifted the curse that had dogged him his whole life. But he hadn't.

And as I watched that shattered soul double over in sorrow, the sky opened up, sheets of hard rain crashing down nearly breaking the ground it hit. Like the gods of irony were showering each of our fated, scripted performances that evening with a round of thunderous applause.

17

❖❖❖❖❖❖❖

I fought to stay conscious as the Saab swerved left then right across two slick lanes. Blood became glue adhering what remained of my clothes to blistering skin.

By the time I hit Munson's car lot, I was done. Harnessing my remaining energy, I pulled in. It wasn't the burns that finished me, it was my chest. Felt like it was being squeezed and I couldn't catch my breath.

Someone had to call the fire department. Someone had to go to the police. Somebody was going to have to get me to a hospital but this dolly was done for the evening.

As my head hung limply out the open window, I saw the juxtaposed street signs of 5th and Vanguard. Like some kind of crazy magnet, this corner. Reminded me of the hitchhiker in that Twilight Zone episode. No matter how far away the girl thinks she's gone, there he is. "Going my way?"

Both ears were ringing while my vision ebbed and flowed. Images came clear then got very white, and disappeared altogether.

Through now useless glasses, it looked to me

like two guys were having a fight at the corner, one holding the other up against a huge Dr. Pepper bottle painted on a stucco wall. That's all I saw before losing consciousness again so I didn't see how the fight turned out.

When my lids lifted, I was staring through the rain at a pair of baby blue polyester trousers. I didn't move but the trousers did. They took a step closer to the car then bent revealing a baby blue polyester jacket and, eventually, a head.

"Doris? Doris, is that you?"

Seemed like I was spending more time with Carroll than with Felix. In fact, every time I was in a jam this drunk showed up. It amuses me to think of him as my spirit guide. This would be just the sort of angel God would reserve for me.

"Doris! Well, what do you know? Whose car you driving tonight?"

"Carroll," I managed to choke out.

Things were only marginally in focus but I could see him. His red maraschino cheeks, bourbon colored eyes, and tobacco-stained teeth were all leaning in toward my blackened mug. The thinning tufts of faded brown hair that I'd only seen anchored back with pomade were now acting as rain gutters down both sides of his neon face.

"Carroll, help me."

He dabbed at a fresh cut on his mouth. The punch must've landed there, the one I never saw thrown. I couldn't manage to ask him about it.

His assessment of my current situation made him swallow hard. "Oh, Bertha," was his summary.

"I don't know where the police are," I squeaked in quiet hysteria as my chin quivered uncontrollably.

"Police. So, you're finally going to turn yourself in. I don't know much but I do know this. The expatriate who I just set straight, the cockroach that just bad-mouthed this great country of ours should turn himself over to the cops, not you. You need a doctor. And I need a drink."

"Carroll, please."

"You're trouble, Doris. Trouble with a capital T."

"I think I'm hurt pretty bad."

With that, I railed forward onto the steering wheel spitting up metallic flavored liquid then pitching myself back against the seat. I picked a brittle clump of hair off of my undaunted jacket lapel, shaking and whimpering like a baby. He reached for my shoulder then changed his mind. He started to leave then changed his mind again. The full import of what was being asked of him finally sank in. He rearranged his belt while looking over the top of my car as if to find some inspiration of his own, and opened the door.

Very gently, he somehow maneuvered me over the center console to the passenger side. I couldn't help him but he persevered. Once that was accomplished and my convulsions ebbed a little, he clenched his fists, slapped on imaginary aftershave to steady himself and turned the key. I passed out.

The tug of his spongy hands brought me back. This brave barfly had me gathered in his arms. Next thing I knew we were ascending concrete steps. I counted the pores on his nose trying to keep alert.

The rain was relentless. Like holy water on demon flesh, I screeched and screeched again each time a droplet found my wounds.

Miraculously, we made it to the top where he put me down, slowly. I wouldn't have guessed him strong enough for any of this but it's hard to tell about people. He had his arm around my good side.

"Can you walk?"

"I think so. Yeah. This the police station?"

"My home away from home."

"Thanks, Carroll. Thank you."

"Yeah. Well, no one has asked me to help with anything for a long time. So don't mention it."

His tiny amber eyes remained focused straight ahead as I studied the hidden emotions radiating behind them. He sounded pretty sober to me.

We entered the all-too-bright building like Siamese twins.

"Wow. Can I help you?" A policeman added support to my unmanned flank.

"Fire."

"Where, miss?"

I gave him limited but accurate directions as the three of us made our way further into the precinct. Then the policeman gave Carroll the once-over.

"Sharkey, isn't it?"

"Carroll Sharkey. That's right."

I didn't feel myself hit the ground.

18
◇◇◇◇◇◇◇

When I woke up, I was in a private hospital room with Felix sitting next to the bed. He looked very tired and stubbly.

"Hey," I gurgled, bandages and pulleys prohibiting any physical contact. He gasped and looked at the door half rising, then reseated himself.

"Hey, baby. Hey now. How you feeling?"

It took a great deal of effort to articulate anything around the throat tube taped to my scabby chin. "How do I look?"

"Beautiful. You look... beautiful, baby."

It was both uncomfortable and heartrending to see him cry. Made me cry too, and we both kind of laughed and cried for a minute. Then he grabbed a tissue and wiped my nose, running a sleeve across his own. Tenderly kissing my forehead between mummy gauze, he sat back down.

"I should call a nurse or something, I think. They've been taking bets on when you'd get around to waking up."

"How bad is it?"

His thumb was wrapped under the armrest while

his gifted fingers nervously pumped imaginary keys above.

"Oh, not too bad, Jules. Not too bad. You lost a little hair in the back there. Little patch of skin, I guess. Word on the street is you were too lucky, Nancy Drew. Kind of goofy for the last three days but..."

"Three days?"

His East Coast tongue moved even more slowly than usual as he carefully gave me his take on things. I've never heard his already bass heavy voice so low.

"You, uh, you went into shock, baby. And, uh, for the past three days you've painted some real wild scenes. All over the place. Talking about that dog you had when you were a kid."

"Bullet."

"Yeah. And about that guy we found in the house a few years ago. And, I don't know, other things. You kept yelling, "Peter, I'm sorry." over and over and over, so, you must've known somebody named Peter is all I could figure."

"Peter."

"Yeah. You were chattering like a frigging monkey half the time but you couldn't hear anybody around you. You never mentioned me. Which is no big deal but I just wanted you to wake up. So I kept talking, trying to make you hear me. I just kept talking to you."

He started to break down again.

"I kept trying to tell you that I'm sorry I wasn't there. And that I...I kept trying to tell you that I love you. But you couldn't hear me."

I reached out my undamaged arm and invited him to take it, which he did.

"I hear you now."

He collected himself as little boys are taught to do.

"Okay. That's real good. Listen, Julie, don't pull this shit again, okay? You're screwing with my chops."

"You played?"

"No, I didn't play. When would I fit this in? I just meant it figuratively, you know. I tried to bring the sax in here but they shut me down."

"I would've liked that."

"Oh, you'd have perked right up. I know that. Charlotte's been here. She sat with me. I need to call her."

"I love Charlotte."

"Yeah? Well maybe you should talk to her a little more often 'cause she didn't know any of this shit."

"I didn't know how to tell her."

"Yeah," He stared off into space then back at me. "I didn't know how to tell her either. Anyway, she knows now."

I've never seen Felix so fragile, so wounded. We smiled and stared, neither sure how to share what was in our hearts.

"What else did the doctors say?"

His foot shuffling turned to delicately chosen words again. "Uh, well, you got some burns, here and there. Nothing that won't get better. Except maybe part of your arm."

He pointed to the arm wrapped in gauze that was suspended by a pulley.

"I remember. Why did it get burnt so badly?"

"I don't know. Maybe something got up your sleeve. Your hand's going to be fine, though. It's more like your wrist and forearm that got the bad ouchy. That burn is pretty deep they tell me."

"My souvenir."

All at once, the tape recorder leapt to mind. That little souvenir could help exonerate me in short order from the battery of questions I would surely be answering soon.

"Felix, where's my coat?"

"In the closet over there."

"Would you check the pockets for me?"

He did. When he brought out the photograph, I got goose bumps. They hurt.

"Let me see it."

He was staring at it as he walked back over to the bed.

"Is this what I think it is?"

"Yeah."

"Jesus, this belongs in a museum, or something. Who took this?"

"A fan. Let me see." I went to readjust myself to take the picture from him, and suffered a rude awakening. "Oooh! Aaagh! Aaagh!"

"Okay, baby. Okay. Take it easy, Spider Girl. You know you're burnt some. Quite a few burns. They've got you on some shit but you're still going to hurt like hell for a while."

I couldn't speak while a billion little knives poked at my legs, which were raised a few inches off the bed, as was my head and arm. Felix put the photograph in my right hand while I took short hard breaths for courage. Eventually, the pain subsided.

"How? How could it survive all that? It's untouched."

"I don't know. But I know that flame-retardant peacoat of yours came in real handy. The doctor says that if you hadn't had it on, you know, sayonara."

"No, I never knew Sinatra."

"What? Jeez. I said sayonara."

The twinkle in my eyes must've given me away. He grinned.

"You think you can play me, Spider Girl? 'Cause you haven't been conscious long enough to be playing anybody."

"Is there a tape recorder in the pocket, too?"

He took the photo from my hand, placed it on the bed stand, and retrieved the recorder. My heart raced.

"Honey, rewind it a little and push play."

The tape was warped from the heat but her voice was audible. Felix threw his hand over his mouth. "Is this a confession?"

"It's an explanation. Better turn it off Felix. Save it for the cops."

He was looking at me hard.

"This is going to be worth something." He put it in his jacket pocket and introspectively laced his fingers behind his head. "I do believe you're going to be famous."

"The hard way. Wait till you see what I've got in the car."

"What's in the car?"

"I'm not sure yet but I'm hoping it's worth the scars."

Felix poured a short glass of water and stuck a flexi-straw in it for me.

"Here, want this?"

I sucked for what seemed like a long while until water finally touched my lips. His brows furrowed.

"Let's celebrate with a little more painkiller, okay? I can only see about a third of your face and that third is making me uneasy. Let me call a nurse." He paused, waiting for approval. He knew this was sticky territory. He knew it had been a long road from junked up to clean. Leaning over the bed, he whispered, "They've already got you on morphine, Jules. That's just what they do in this kind of situation. We can deal with it later, when you're feeling better."

Little did he know I'd been thinking about taking a little painkiller for the past several days. And I could have found another reason, if not for the fire, but it would've been harder to rationalize. I mean, who would begrudge a burn patient anything? I'll be forever grateful that the choice was taken out of my hands. Besides, I really was in a lot of pain.

"Yeah, dad. Thanks."

19

◇◇◇◇◇◇

Right after a nurse had administered some Demerol, a doctor walked in. "Well, what have we here?" she chuckled in doctorly fashion. "Welcome back."

This young woman was Dr. Stewart, an affable back-home blonde with no obvious burns on her willowy legs or sun-kissed cheeks. Still, she exuded a believable amount of intellect that transcended her annoying lack of damage.

She gently explained that she was my new psychiatrist and that she would be available to me throughout my recovery and for as long as I felt I needed her. I've never been big on sharing personal exposition with perfect strangers but I'm no idiot, this skirt could issue the drugs. I would not lose her number.

A nurse checked my vitals while Dr. Stewart filled me in on my physical condition. Though Dr. Stewart was a mere shrink, she was able to offer a bit more medical expertise than Felix had provided. The nurse left but the doctor remained, leaning attentively over the metal bed railing. It was her educated guess that I would be able to go home in four or five days now that I was with it, if everything remained status quo.

Fortunately, these were second-degree burns, not third.

It was also Dr. Stewart's opinion that I'd be cranky for quite awhile and that I was to ask for a shot of Demerol whenever I felt it necessary. I promised her that I would.

"I'll see you tomorrow, Julie. I'm going to go let Dr. Herman know that you're back among the living. Get some rest. Felix, you too."

She patted his shoulder allowing her flawless hand to rest there until he looked at her. The consolation seemed somehow too familiar.

"Thanks. I'll do that," he responded politely.

"Well, see to it that you do or I'll have to get tough," she purred while cocking her doll head. I knew this bitch. I'd met her a million times backstage at his concerts. Not always this well turned out, but it was her. And for one dark moment I thought I saw writing on the wall though I wasn't going to let myself go there, not happy as I was to be alive.

As Dr. Stewart turned to leave, a strapping, thirty-something fellow wearing a white cotton button-down with the cuffs rolled twice passed her in the doorway. His tie hung to the left and down a couple of inches from its appropriate position. He averted his eyes in a shy kind of stance as he brushed past the good doctor.

"Yes? Can I help you?" she asked.

"Police, ma'am. DiAngelo, Detective Francis Di-Angelo. I spoke to Dr. Herman earlier. And yesterday, too."

"I see. Well, this patient shouldn't have any visitors right now. Can't this wait until tomorrow?" She spoke like a doctor but tossed her hair like a shampoo model.

"No, ma'am, I don't think so. Miss Page is the key figure in what's looking like a pretty complicated situation. I've got a few questions for her."

The doctor's lightly mascarad lashes batted twice. He tried again.

"It'll only take a minute. Five minutes tops."

After considering his request, and generous mouth, she acquiesced. "Just keep it brief, Detective. Miss Page needs her rest. And don't upset her. We just got her back. Understood?"

"Yes ma'am."

Felix leapt to his feet to either give the guy his chair or show him that he was much taller. The detective extended one big paw for Felix to shake.

"Hi. Detective DiAngelo. Frank DiAngelo. Mr. Page?"

"No. No, man. Felix Mint."

"You related here, Mr. Mint?"

Felix had been nodding since this guy walked in. Nodding his head like someone was telling him a story. Now that the guy was actually talking to him directly Felix continued to nod maybe a full five seconds after the question had been asked.

"You let people call you Francis?"

Detective DiAngelo heard the ancient tribal bell being rung and jumped into the pit with Felix.

"Yeah. Yeah, I let people call me Francis. Some people. What do people call you? To your face?"

Felix laughed while rubbing his chin. Detective DiAngelo smiled broadly while adjusting the roll of both cuffs and shifting his solid weight from one foot to the other.

"Look, Sergeant Friday, I don't think my girl-friend is in the mood to do this right now. Why don't you come back later?"

"This is police business, pal. I'm going to have to ask you to leave."

"Oh, I don't think so. You just do whatever it is that you do and I'll be right over here." Felix sat on a plastic-covered bench under the window, pulled his hat over his forehead, and crossed his arms.

The detective slowly turned his head to me but his eyes stayed on Felix as long as possible. When both men had figuratively pissed on every tree in the room, we got down to business.

Detective DiAngelo's substantial thighs spread across the seat of a hard-back chair. He tucked his bargain basement loafers under it, resting them on the bends of its hollow metal frame.

He looked like a boxer. He looked like a guy who'd coach Little League. He looked like he might get a little too physical if he had a little too much to drink and he looked like he loved his mom.

I could smell Italian food on his heavy breath as he repositioned himself and the chair close enough for us to talk intimately.

What the morphine alone could not accomplish, the Demerol chaser did, creating an altered, centered, peaceful space in my head. A space I'd missed for a very long time. The almost overwhelming pain had dramatically subsided and I felt wonderful, lost in a soft, dreamy, narcotic fog.

"Miss Page, I'm Frank DiAngelo. I'm the detective assigned to your case." He flashed me his badge while introducing himself. "Okay if I ask you some questions?"

"How's Carroll?"

"What?"

"The man who brought me to the station, what happened to him?"

"Carroll Sharkey?" The detective chuckled. "He's quite a character, isn't he?"

"He saved my life."

"That's right, he did. Well, once we determined that his condition had nothing to do with yours, Lieutenant Korst drove him back to his car and followed him home. He's fine, miss. How you doing?"

"I'm okay. How's the house?"

"The house, right. Parts of the place are gutted. Other parts held together pretty well. From the outside, you wouldn't know anything happened. Fire's funny that way. The rain kept things from getting out of hand. That was a lucky break. Say, you've got a lot of questions yourself, don't you? That makes sense."

"How's Peter?"

Felix adjusted his butt but not his hat when I asked after Peter.

"We took Mr. Common into custody that night and transferred him to the Willowcrest Rehab Center and Sanitarium on 73rd. He wasn't doing very well. We told him we could get him into a witness protection program if he could come up with some information that we needed and he's been real cooperative. I don't think he has any strong sense of allegiance to those creeps after what happened, so we cut him a deal."

The detective fingered his collar, unbuttoned one more button, and leaned in close to my right ear like he didn't want Felix to hear.

"Look Miss Page, I'm gonna have to ask you the

questions or my boss is gonna get real mad. Go easy. I just got this promotion to detective. This is my first time with anything like this."

"Sorry. Me, too."

We smiled at each other from close range, kissing distance apart. Detective DiAngelo leaned against the back of the chair crossing both paws over the crotch of his olive drab chinos.

The drugs had loosened my tongue. "They had Sandy killed you know. That's what knocked her over the top."

He shot straight up in the chair, whipping out a ballpoint pen from his shirt pocket and cheap spiral notepad from somewhere behind him, south of his gun.

"We're talking about Sander Harper?"

"When you guys found him in the wash behind the power plant, Maxine decided to take matters into her own hands. Nobody was supposed to get hurt. She liked Sandy. I liked Sandy."

"We only found a bike, Miss Page. We never found a body."

"Are you saying he's alive?"

The detective looked up sharply, then straightened his tie. "I'm saying we didn't find a body. How well did you know him?"

"I didn't know him, know him. I just talked to him whenever I bought a soda or a pack of smokes."

"You know you shouldn't smoke."

"Yeah. Just look at me."

"Hey, I'm sorry," he stammered, realizing the irony in his reprimand.

"It's okay. What do you want to know, detective?"

My head was swimming in a river of Demerol, swimming and swimming.

"Sure. Again, sorry. Uh, I guess the primary thing we want to figure out is what your interest is here, Miss Page. How did you get involved with Miss Montego in the first place? And what did you see, if anything, during the fire?"

"I saw everything."

"Excellent. There was another body exhumed from the fire. Can you identify him?"

"Happy Man."

"Right. Anything else?"

"There's a boat. His people are waiting for him on a boat."

"Actually, the bad guys showed up right after the good guys did. We've impounded the ship, Miss Page. So, you can explain the connection between Miss Montego and Mr. Pungpapong?"

Felix joined in the conversation from under his hat in a successful attempt to make me laugh.

"What was that name, Francis?"

The cop answered Felix but kept his eyes on me. "Pungpapong. Thongchai Pungpapong."

"Tongue tie Powpong?"

"Thongchai..."

"Tough guy Ping Pong?"

"I'm not talking to you, pal."

"But what does this have to do with Sinatra?"

"Are you all right, miss?"

The small laughter emanating from inside the bandages must've sounded like a cow lowing.

"Detective, did you know that Maxine Montego used to be a songwriter?"

My head tilted over to Felix. When our eyes met,

he responded by getting up and walking over to the bed as if I'd asked him to. Silently, I guess I had.

"No, ma'am. I understood she worked on a TV show of some kind."

Clearly, he didn't know a thing about Maxine.

Felix felt the need to cut in for real at this point.

"Everything you need is right here, Francis." He handed DiAngelo the recorder. "Be careful with it. It's already damaged from the heat."

"What's this?"

"That's Maxine's confession," Felix answered, followed by an addendum from me.

"Everything that happened before and during the fire is on that tape. I recorded the whole thing, at Maxine's request."

"You've got to be kidding me."

DiAngelo paced in front of Felix then scooped up the recorder with the urgency and tenderness of a mother snatching her baby back from a kidnapper's arms.

There was something about this big Boy Scout, something dark or manic or, I don't know, an edge that was vaguely unsettling. Add to that his sweet approach and brutish good looks and you've got yourself one complex copper. I decided I liked him. Of course, I was loaded at the time.

With the tape recorder in hand and an understanding that there would be further conversations, Frank DiAngelo felt he had enough ammunition to take to his superiors.

On his way to the door, he reiterated how sorry he was about my recent experience. Then, just like in the movies, he said he'd be back tomorrow and to not leave town. I chose to believe he was being funny. Ciao, bella detectivo.

In the days that followed, I was visited by several of Berle's finest, including Francis. I approached each visit with a tremendous amount of resolve and a great flush of Demerol, which made everything absolutely doable.

As my release date grew closer, a nurse asked Felix to bring in a turban or bandanna so I could go home without thinking about the back of my bald pate.

I sent him to Wanda's House of Hair, which is not only a busy local salon but also serves as the neighborhood's premier wig distributor and beauty supply shop. They would have a turban.

He brought me a white one, much like the kind Elizabeth Taylor and Lana Turner wore when they suffered a bad-hair day. The one Felix picked was especially special with pearlescent quarter-size sequins sewn throughout the terry cloth. I wasn't anticipating those. I thought how perhaps the glistening sequins might keep people from noticing the seeping blisters punctuating my singed face. Hey, at least he remembered to bring something.

The big day finally came without much ceremony. It wasn't like I hadn't seen myself without the bandages already. I made sure to see every spongy, yellow scab developing along the way.

Felix had just helped get me into some old clothes and my glittering turban when Frank came by to wish me well. Frank had developed some paternal attachment to me during my hospital stay, one that extended beyond diamonds and dead bodies. Couldn't've been my looks, unless there's some bandage fetish I'm unaware of.

I think it was a control thing. Felix wasn't doing a good enough job in his eyes. He made that clear every chance he got. And truth to tell, things had gotten a little icy between Felix and I, mostly over Dr. Honey Pie. But the bandages were off and I was alive. Ultimately, it was a fine day.

Felix placed my peacoat around my shoulders while a nurse helped me into a wheelchair. Before I'd escaped, the phone rang. Felix picked it up.

"Hello? Who? Holy cow, really? Yeah, sure, just a sec." He started to hand the phone to me.

"Who is calling me here?"

He continued to extend the receiver. "It's Sprint. They want to talk to you about changing your long-distance coverage. Take it already."

"This is Julie."

"Hello! Julie! Thank God you're okay. My name is Veronica Long. I'm with Random House, Inc. How are you doing?

"Excuse me, did you say you were with Random House?"

"We're interested in talking to you about your story, Maxine's story. Not now, of course. I just wanted to touch base with you. We called the day they brought you to the hospital. Pretty touch and go there for awhile, huh?"

"You called before?"

"Well, we couldn't find out much but we knew where you were and that you were holding steady. Anyway, we think you've got one hell of a story to tell. And, Julie, if there's anything we can do to help you out over the next few weeks, please don't hesitate to call me, okay?"

"Random House?"

She laughed. "They tell me you're a writer, Julie. You must've heard of us. We're pretty big. We own most of the others."

So, I was about to be published. That meant I was going to have to write a book. I remembered what Maxine had told me. Burning is easy, it's healing that's a bitch.

20

◇◇◇◇◇◇◇

As a nurse pushed me in an unnecessary wheel-chair through a labyrinth of corridors, I kept rubbing the frayed left cuff of the navy coat that, along with Carroll, had saved my life.

Vicodin replaced Demerol at the hospital pharmacy on the way out. Nothing wrong with Vicodin. My motto has always been 'Where there's a pill, there's a way.'

Felix had the Plymouth double-parked right outside but the cameras and microphones made the short journey exhausting. Several over-eager reporters fell in step with us vying for attention as we elbowed our way from the automatic glass doors to the car. I'd figured on a little press but couldn't have imagined how out of control the media would get.

Once we turned onto Poppy, I breathed a sigh of relief. Felix awkwardly helped me out of the car and into the front room. There were messages from two other publishing houses on the answering machine. Book deals were being discussed and advances alluded to. There was a message from the newspaper, as well. They felt I owed them an exclusive and asked that I call as soon as I got settled in. Seemed the circus bosses couldn't even wait for me to take off my shoes before they'd all pitched their tents.

I shuffled to the bathroom to reconsider my wounds in my own environment. The bathroom light was unforgiving. I did what I could with the hair remaining but decided the smartest thing to do would be to cut it all off. Start over. It'd give me a chance to find out what my natural color is.

Felix had made a strong pot of coffee by the time I emerged from the bathroom somewhat refreshed and very glad to be home. As I gingerly sat down on the couch, I noticed Maxine's suitcase of charms tucked under the kitchen table. Seeing it reminded me of how it came into my unlikely possession. It reminded me of Sandy. It reminded me of watching her shoot herself in the mouth. When I came to, Felix was sitting on the coffee table in front of me squeezing my good hand and shouting, "Julie! Julie, wake up! Wake up!"

"Hey."

"Hey, now, baby. You want to go to bed for awhile?"

"No, I'm okay. Did you open it when you brought it home?"

"The suitcase? Nah. We had a deal."

"Let's do it."

Reluctantly, he helped me into the kitchen and threw the suitcase up on the table. We both tried to ignore the dried blood staining one side.

The contents were everything I'd hoped for, perhaps Maxine's entire body of work spanning the better part of two decades, from Vegas to her early retirement.

Neatly stacked to the left of a useless leather

strap buckled straight down the center were several albums, all of them hers. Stacks of 45s took up the right side, some Capitol releases, some less prestigious labels. Then around and on top of the records were pictures, lots and lots of pictures. Her life with Peter documented in touching detail. At Sardi's, at The Brown Derby, in a studio, on a stage. Other photographs containing couples whose names I'd never know captured forever the camping trips and barbecues, beach parties and poker games that make up a life. So many snapshots. They looked so young and happy.

And there were famous people, too. One of her and Jackie Wilson in front of the Five Four Ballroom. One of her and Lenny Bruce dancing in front of her band; Peter at the piano casting a comically evil eye on the swinging twosome. Another with Rosemary Clooney, Dinah Washington and Maxine all sporting hats and gloves with shopping bags over their arms and great big smiles on their mugs strolling down some nameless boulevard.

Under the vinyl were promotional posters and news clippings including those centered on the fire at the Robertson Supper Club in 1967, and in the satin pouch on the inside of the lid were several copyright papers as well as her birth certificate. Apparently, she had been born Bridget Maxine Monty at Holy Innocence Hospital in L.A. County. I'd be adding a copy of her death certificate to finish off the personal portfolio she'd left to me.

It's funny how well I felt I knew Maxine after studying the contents of her suitcase, mostly because of what she chose to gather as the sum of her life in the days before her death. Nothing about a mobster boyfriend, nothing to suggest her run as a television host, no books for the blind. It was all about music.

It might sound morbid or masochistic, but after perusing her mementos, I felt particularly proud and glad to have such pronounced scars from traveling with this muse. I'm not the kind of gal who believes scars are necessarily a bad thing. To me, they're a visible reminder of the pain we choose to keep, humbling us, holding us accountable.

I went to replace the documents and felt a small box in the bottom of the pouch. It was a small heart shaped box made of varnished cardboard and pressed flowers. In the box was a ring, at least a three-carat diamond, marquise cut and set in smooth yellow gold. Audrey Hepburn classic. It was also probably cubic zirconium. What were the chances of anybody having a diamond that size? Except perhaps a jewel thief's fence.

Felix and I looked at each other and then at the ring half a dozen times before we spoke.

"It's probably just a favorite cocktail ring of hers."

"It's probably the last of the Montego Supremes. You've got to get it appraised."

"Yeah." I slid it on the scabless middle finger of my left hand. It still hurt to move that wrist but the ring fit perfectly. "Felix..."

"Don't go there."

"But..."

"Julie, come on. You could retire on what that ring is worth if it's real. Get it appraised."

"I'd rather not know."

"There you go." He lit a smoke and shook his head.

"This will be like my medal of valor. You can't put a price on something like that."

"Nancy Drew would want to know."

When the phone rang, Felix picked it up. It was Doctor Stewart. He assured her that I was doing fine, that we were just getting settled in. The end of the conversation went like this, "Okay, Margie, I will. No, honey, thank you. Yeah, I'm fine. Oh, that's sweet. Okay, I'll call you later. Bye-bye."

There was a moment of silence between us that had become all too common over the past several days. I chose to break it.

"Margie, huh?"

"Jules, come on."

"I can't do this right now, Felix. My self-image is fairly battered as it is.

"There's nothing going on."

"Don't patronize me, you selfish bastard. I've been here before, remember? Just wait until my hair grows back, can you do that?"

"That was three years ago. You weren't even moved in yet. Jeez, baby, are you ever gonna let that go?"

"How can I? Every groupie you fuck keeps it fresh in my mind."

He turned his head quickly to the left as if he'd been slapped.

"I'm going through some shit with this, too, you know. She's concerned about both of us. She's a sweet kid."

"Jesus Christ," I muttered under my breath. "May I have some more coffee?" He refilled both cups.

I took a long drink then seized the opportunity to bring up a much bigger issue I'd been chewing on in the hospital. What had been building and graciously ignored since I met Maxine really had to be discussed now that I was home and the real work about to begin.

"Felix, we have to talk about how I'm going to go about writing this book. I'm going to need some space."

"Space. Right." He picked up his sax from the counter behind him and started blowing taps. Then he put it down and laced his fingers on the table. "I've been wondering how this would come down. So, tell me. How are we going to do this?"

I picked at a hard black scab on my knee. "I'm not sure exactly."

He crossed his legs, turning his head to stare into the front room, as if something in there was worth watching. I took a pill and went to bed.

In the morning, he presented me with cappuccino, biscotti, and a beautiful bouquet of wild flowers. "How'd you sleep?"

"Like I was drugged. You?"

"Oh, you know, on and off. I love you, Jules."

"I know you do."

"So, do we still have to talk about space then?"

I've never loved anyone the way I love Felix. I'm sure I never will. He anchors me. He fascinates me. He towers over me in every way, and that's a problem.

When we met, all I wanted was to be lost in him, and that was easy to do. In fact, I couldn't find myself at all whenever he was around. Mostly I created this. Sometimes he wanted me to feel that way. But even when he put me in my place I didn't mind too much.

Back then, I didn't have anything else going for me, and besides, we are talking about Felix Mint.

Sex with him became a nightly exorcism, every devil feeding on my worthlessness was sent to the cornfield for whatever amount of time his miraculous hands were on me. I transcended mortality when watching him play. The stains on his shirts gave me purpose. Each of his rather pronounced imperfections made him all the more perfect through my thick, corrective lenses.

I've never doubted his love for me; his fidelity, absolutely, but never his love, constant and cool. I couldn't always rationalize from whence it came but then I would remember that, for whatever reason, I'd been his muse. I just always figured he'd be the one to leave. As it turns out, it was going to be me.

I had to leave for a while or I'd never write again. All the Dr. Stewart's aside, I couldn't produce anything important there, not in the light of his brilliance, not in the brilliance of his shadow. Not when I spent so much time admiring how uniquely he sat and dressed and took in air.

I had to leave, for a little while, until I finished the book. The creative process can be an extremely selfish one sometimes. Well, every time.

The day after I got home, I gave the newspaper their story along with my resignation. I was front-page news by the evening edition. I'd say that trumps a farewell cake in the conference room.

Over the next couple of weeks, Felix patiently took care of me and even helped me pack as we decided what would come with me and what would stay there till I moved back. During this process, we hashed things out.

"It won't be long, Felix. I just can't write here."

"Because of her?"

"No, because of me."

"Because you love me too much, right?"

"Don't do that. You know what I'm talking about."

"Yeah, I do. I do know what you're talking about and this sucks. You are my lucky charm, baby. Magically delicious. You go, it goes. I mean, this is not just impacting me on a sex, dinner, laundry level, okay? You're fucking with my chops."

"So your desire to keep me here is mercenary, not emotional."

"Oooh, so your desire to keep me here is mercenary, not emoootional. What is that crap? You watched way too much of that Opra in the hospital, you know that?"

"You're a real asshole sometimes, you know that?"

"Well, you're a whore."

"A whore. I'm a whore."

"Sure."

"You're the one who can't keep it in your pants."

"Okay, let it go."

"No, I want to know. On what are you basing that insult?"

As his own words turned against him, he began to deflate.

"I don't know. It just sounded, you know, strong. Hey, here's an idea for your big book. 'Men are from Mercenary – Women are from Emoootional.'"

We went around and around like that for days. Felix changed my bandages, made the coffee, and bought me cigarettes while each scab gradually fell away. He brought home boxes and I wondered where the hell I thought I was going.

21

❖❖❖❖❖❖

The first place I drove by myself was to visit Peter at the Willowcrest Rehabilitation Center and Sanitarium. It was easy to find his room with all the armed guards around it. Getting clearance to see him had been procured prior to my visit. He looked a little gaunt and his head made a slight shoofly jerk every so often. He had the shakes pretty bad, too, but seemed comfortable enough in that institutional blue cotton robe. He even said he was happy to see me, which was a surprise in that he hadn't liked me much during our one and only face-to-face.

Willowcrest was to be his home until the authorities transported him into the witness protection program, at which time he would be given a new name and relocated to parts unknown. When I asked him how he felt about living out his days in a witness protection program he was quick to tell me he liked the idea. No more criminals. No more club managers. Hopefully, no more mistakes. I said that it sounded great but I was thinking what a bleak, isolating conclusion it was going to make to an unsatisfying life.

I didn't know how to tell him that I had inherited his partner's music catalogue but that was the point of my visit so I drummed up the courage and spit it out. Strangely enough, he didn't care.

"No one's touched that catalogue for years, kid," he said off-handedly. "Knock yourself out. See what you can do with it."

When I told him about the suitcase, however, he was fascinated. Said he'd really like to take that with him and asked if he could. I said yes though I was thinking that there was no way in hell I was going to give up that suitcase until the book was finished.

He had a lot of questions. I tried to answer them. I guess the fact that I'd been with her when she died created some small bond between Peter and myself, though he still wasn't clear on why I'd popped into their lives at the last minute like I did. I could explain my involvement to the cops. It was harder to explain it to this man.

After all, Peter had the most shattered investment of anyone. He'd watched his nerve, purpose, and best friend go up in smoke - twice. He knew things I would never know about happy men and losing babies and maintaining one's brilliance by choosing to stay underground. Not that he had done that, but he understood it. He'd studied it for years.

Just when I thought he'd run out of questions, he asked one more. He wanted to know what I thought the odds were on the cops letting him have a memorial service for Maxine, maybe in a week or so, when he felt a little stronger. "You think the cops would let me do something like that in my current incarcerated condition, and all?" I said I'd make a call and see what we could do. I liked the idea, too.

I called Frank from the room. He listened as I made my case for such a service and for the authorities allowing Peter to attend the service before they sent him away.

As I heard myself ask permission, I realized how ridiculous I sounded. The guy was going into a witness protection program, for fuck's sake. Even his hospital bed was surrounded by guns. Nobody was going to allow him to attend a public service, especially one that would, no doubt, be buggy with cameras and reporters. Nobody, that is, except Frank DiAngelo.

After a long pause on the other end of the receiver, Frank spoke.

"Okay, Julie. Okay, yeah, let's do that. That sounds nice. You make the arrangements and I'll take care of the rest. Yeah, she deserves a nice going away party. Maybe Mr. Common does, too. We'll get him set up with his new identity directly after the service. When he leaves there, he leaves for good. That works. How you holding up?"

I gave him an update on my health and thanked him profusely for saying yes when I was so sure he was going to say no. Peter was a little taken aback, as well, but eager to start making plans.

He told me who to call. He was lucid. He had names. He also asked me to get him a suit for the occasion, a tux, if I wouldn't mind. He said I should just use some of the money I'd be making off of the music catalogue to cover it. I grinned and said I would do that.

I got up to leave but Peter wasn't ready to let me go. I sat on the edge of the bed wondering what else we could possibly have to talk about.

He sat next to me.

"You mind staying a few more minutes? This place is kind of…it's kind of lonely in here."

We discussed music in general and the old Vegas Strip, Ben Frank's and the Home Shopping Network. Then, he got to talking about Maxine.

"When I hooked up with Maxine she was working at the Stork Club and singing songs like I'd never heard. I joined her band a month later and a month after that, we were living together in a one bedroom flat on 163rd.

These chick songwriters today, man, they've never even heard of Maxine Montego but it was gals like Max who broke ground for these kids, with the writing and arranging and producing and shit.

A big male nurse came in and handed Peter some pills, which he took, then cleared his throat and continued.

"My God, we had a ball. She had Los Angeles by the ass. Every jukebox from here to the border had her stocked, and the trades all wanted to know who she was seeing." He turned to the nurse who had remained to take his blood pressure. "For the record, she was seeing me."

The nurse grinned without making eye contact with either of us, removed the inflatable sleeve, and split.

When the old man started talking again, his voice cracked more often and his pauses got a little longer.

"Kid, she had an extraordinary life. I was lucky to bully my way into it. You were, too." I nodded as he patted my hand. "You wouldn't believe what that woman could fall into one trip at a time. But it was always an adventure, good ones, bad ones," he rose and walked across the room to a box of Kleenex. "And if it weren't for Maxine, I'd have jumped off a bridge a long time ago out of sheer boredom. I owe her plenty. Best times I remember have all been with Maxine."

He blew his nose and wiped his eyes before breaking the bittersweet mood. "Don't get me wrong. She could be a real bitch."

My mouth fell open and for a second we just stared at each other, then I started to laugh. It was only me in the audience, but Peter was really working the room, as they say.

"It's true. Sometimes she was a bitch, sometimes she was terribly kind. So, what are you going to do? Maxine Montego was a woman, a rebel, and an innovator, not always in that order. But she knew exactly who she was at every moment. I can't say that for too many people. Everything about her was amplified, her humor, her pain. And she was the most focused writer I've ever known. Watching her work was a privilege."

I could feel myself tearing up. He walked back over to the bed and handed me a tissue.

"You know, these last few years Max sold jewelry on the television and the jewelry these people sell isn't real. It's about selling stuff that looks so much like the real thing you can't tell the difference. And I think that's sort of what's wrong with the world today. People can't tell the difference. I'm not even sure people care. But let me just say, for the record, Maxine Montego, whatever else she was, was the real thing. And she was, for the record, the love of my life. You put that in your book, okay?"

"Yes, sir. I promise."

It was hard to listen to Peter knowing that he wouldn't be seen again after the service. I thought how I was glad I hadn't gotten to know him any better. He would've grown on me. There were enough similarities between him and I, Maxine and Felix that we evidently had plenty to talk about. It was nice.

As I hugged him goodbye and started to leave, he touched my elbow. I turned back around.

"Kid, that Caddy out there, it meant a whole lot to Max. I shouldn't take it with me. It wouldn't be prudent under the circumstances. Will you take it? And not sell it? You know, drive it? Would you do that for Max?"

Tearing up again, I said I would be honored.

Over the next week, pink slips were passed and papers signed. I would be handing him a suitcase and he would be handing me car keys at the memorial service, which I was busy planning as his proxy.

Meanwhile, the publishing houses were implacable in their bids for my attention. I chose one based on who was willing to fork over the fattest advance so I could rent a place to stay while writing the book. The battle over me had nothing to do with literature, you understand. This was just Corporate America clamoring to make a score and enjoy what would inevitably be a fast, juicy profit on the sensational story de jour.

I secured a furnished apartment in the Village near where I'd sold the dead frogs. My Hermes 3000 typewriter was already there along with all of my earthly possessions, which only required one wardrobe crate and eight cardboard boxes. The place was drab and a little moist from existing so close to the ocean, but at least I would have a roof over my fuzzy head.

I, like Peter, would be leaving from the mortuary to a new location. Felix would drive me to the service in the Plymouth. I'd drive away in the Cadillac. Everything had been taken care of. Nothing to do now but go.

"You okay?"

"Yeah. Sure. You okay?"

"Oh, yeah, you know, I've been digging out some old phone numbers. I'll do okay. Hey, some girls think I'm the one that got away."

"I'll be gone for, like, six months. We'll see each other. I'm not leaving you, damn it. I'm just writing a book. I'm not leaving."

He walked around the table.

"Then where are your things?"

"So, by threatening me with other women I'll want to stay? That's your angle?"

"It ain't why. It just is."

"Wow. Well then, I'm not sure we had anything worth worrying about."

"Who's worried? Are you ready?"

"Here. Let me fix your cufflink. Can you get this for me?"

I handed him my pearls and lifted the hair of my burgundy wig. He fastened the delicate clasp. As I started to pull away, he grabbed my shoulders and turned me around.

"Julie, I'm just going to say this once because for all I know we won't be talking like this again."

He hadn't even said what was on his mind and wet mascara was already running down my cheeks.

"Okay. When we met, I knew you'd been through some shit. I could see it in the way you looked so hopeful every time you saw me. Like maybe I could save you. Like I was some kind of big man. You know, getting laid is easy, and I've been pretty lucky at getting stroked professionally, but nobody ever made me feel like if I would just be there for them they'd be okay. And I don't know if I helped you get out of a jam or not. But I do know that thinking I did made me want to be there. It gave me a sense of responsibility for the first time in my life and it even made me want to play better. And I did. And I have for the last three years or so. And I know it's selfish of me to not want you to go off and get famous and sleep somewhere else while you're doing it but I liked it when you needed me. Okay? That's my problem, all right? You don't need me now, and I'm not good with that. And as far as fucking other women goes, it means nothing. It's just what men do when they don't know how to proceed."

That's when I pulled away from him in attentive disgust. He continued.

"From the horse's ass, baby, it's true. You know, like, if I fuck her, I'll feel better. If I fuck her, I'll really hurt the woman who is actually ripping my heart out of my chest. Every fuck, for those few minutes, I'm valuable."

"Felix, please shut up. You're so not helping."

"Well, I'm not good at talking about this shit so, that's it. I've got a problem. You don't have a problem, I do. And I'm hoping that we can work something out because I'm so fucking angry about all of this. And that's all. That's what I wanted to say."

I pulled out the handkerchief sticking from his jacket pocket and blew my nose. "Felix, we have other problems."

"Do we not talk enough? Where is this shit coming from? What other problems do we have, Julie?"

"Like I've given you way too much control over my life. Like you can giveth or taketh away with a glance or a single remark. That's not right. We need to reevaluate the balance of power between us, something more equitable. I need that. And that's my problem, not yours. Look, I've walked through fire and leaving you for a few months is harder. This is the hardest thing I've ever done. I'm trying to stand up, Felix. If you love me, you've got to let me stand up."

"This whole thing is fucked."

"It's going to work out."

"When?"

"When I finish – writing – the book."

22
◇◇◇◇◇◇

Maxine Montego – the name was plastered everywhere as the media continued their brutal quest for truth (or something better) regarding the whole ugly thing. People who thought she'd died years ago were dumbfounded. People who watched her every day on the Home Shopping Network were horrified. Even the people who had never heard of her knew all about her now. At least they thought they did.

There was a mob waiting when Felix and I got to the service. Peter stood on the steps amidst a handful of cops in suits and sunglasses who were already wandering in and out of the Palmdale Mortuary on Avenue D. News crews were unloading their vans and setting up shop along the wide cement stairway that led to two sets of double doors. I stepped out of my shoe while trying to hurry up those steps. That was unfortunate. A couple of reporters got so close to me that I had a hard time bending down to pick it up. And their continued badgering with questions like, "Tell us about the fire?" and "What were her last words?" set the tone for the day.

Before I made it into the building, a young Asian man, twenty, maybe a little older, with porcelain skin, smooth, jet black hair and the most extraordinary almond shaped eyes I've ever seen came barreling up through the professional stalkers and looked me right in the eye. He seemed so harried and panic-stricken that I actually leaned into his gaze, waiting to see if I could help in some way. Then he stepped back smiling, pulled a camera from his pocket, and shot me at close range, disappearing into the bulging crowd.

Yeah, it was odd. People are odd. My mug had been pasted all over the TV for the past three weeks. I thought perhaps he saw the service as a kind of roadside attraction and wanted to take something with him to show the folks back home.

Observing this, a cop approached and suggested I go inside. No one but Peter, Felix, the cops, and me were allowed in the sitting room at present. I double-checked that everything had been arranged as planned.

White lilies and orchids lined each pew as well as the podium. No small expense, but Peter wanted them. He also wanted candles, lots and lots of candles. I couldn't think of anything more inappropriate but had honored his wishes. White candles of varying sizes flickering softly across the altar and a baby grand had been wheeled in and blanketed with an extraordinary assortment of photographs depicting the woman of the hour.

Walking together toward the foyer, I told Peter how beautiful everything looked and asked how he was holding up. He stepped back and opened his arms. "How do I look?" With his hair shining silver, black tux and bow tie, he looked like somebody famous, like somebody who belonged next to Maxine Montego, but his eyes reflected nothing but horror and sadness and guilt.

"You look so handsome, Peter."

Taking my hand, he assured me he was fine. "I'm going to go back out there now and see what's going on."

"Peter, I've got the suitcase in the Plymouth. I'll get it to Detective DiAngelo right after the service before you leave. Is that good?"

"Sure, kid. That sounds great. Oh, hey, here are the keys to the Cad."

He handed them off as if it wasn't breaking his heart to do so, but I knew better.

"Thanks, Peter. I'm going to take really good care of it."

He considered my pledge. "Yeah, I believe you will."

Then he turned his attention to the small army of cops who continued to position themselves in and around the building. "Man, they've got this place locked down tight." He looked up at me grinning. "I must be one scary sonofabitch."

"I know, huh? Well, they're just doing they jobs, I suppose."

"Tight as a drunk on Christmas, this place is. This is some crazy shit."

I nodded in agreement as the mortuary staff opened the doors. He made his way back outside and as people walked up the steps he greeted each with a handshake or kiss on the cheek, like a champion, rising gracefully to the occasion. You were right, Maxine, I observed. The show goes on.

Peter knew that everybody there felt a little embarrassed for him, embarrassed by the irony of it all. The press had latched on to the fact that this was the man who had ditched Maxine in a burning building a few decades ago, and here he was again. But he wasn't about to let any of that keep him from taking care of her now.

As I stepped back out onto the cement steps, I saw Charlotte and made my way past the cables and microphones to say hi.

"Char, look at this mess. Who are these people?"

"Well, the appliquéd tops and bejeweled accent watches have to belong to HSN dignitaries. That's my guess. These other folks, I'm not sure. But with all this press, you can bet there are more than a few publicity hounds out here. I'm going to go get a seat before there aren't any seats to be got. Hang tough, honey."

Charlotte squeezed my arm and went inside. Kevin Quinlin was holding court at the opposite end of the steps talking to a reporter with a tearful Tammy Duke at his side.

From just beyond them, I saw Peter step around the building with an unlit smoke hanging from his lips feeling his tux jacket for a light. Frank brushed past me and started toward him but Peter came back around the corner in a hurry with a cop directly behind him. Before Frank cleared my reach, I grabbed the sleeve of his coat.

"Frank, I have a suitcase that belongs to Mr. Common out front. Can you wait a minute for me to go get it?"

"I'm sorry, Julie, but this crowd is getting a little out of hand. We need to get him in there and get this thing started if we're going to do it. Don't worry about the suitcase. I'll take care of it."

Then he bent down and spoke softly near my cheek like he had in the hospital room. "He won't mind waiting a couple more days. The guy's got nothing but time."

I stepped into the parlor and stood to the side of the pews. Felix joined me. In silence, we stared straight ahead at the double doors as people came in and seated themselves. After a couple minutes of this, I curtly asked if he'd moved the suitcase from the Plymouth to the Cad. He said he had, tossing me the look of disgust that had become his regular way of looking at me over the last few days.

Then a single shot rang out.

Felix threw himself over me on instinct, pinning us both to the nearest wall. The chattering crowd fell dumb, frozen in disbelief. When the second shot was fired, everyone ran for their lives. Felix tried to pull me to the ground behind a pew but I broke free and reeled around in time to see several policemen draw their guns as they darted through the doors leading to the lobby. I ran toward the action and found it.

As if in slow-motion, I watched one cop attempting to keep the old man's heart beating by bashing on his chest as another was yelling very near his face, "Hold on, Peter. Can you hear me? Hold on. Hold on." Then, they both stopped trying.

There was another guy lying limp next to him. A guy maybe in his fifties, Asian, well-dressed. It only took one bullet to put him down, too. Frank put his gun back in his shoulder holster. Standing behind the dead men was the kid who took my picture before the service, the kid with the almond shaped eyes. He was handcuffed now, looking lost, his beautiful eyes fixed on the blood as it ran together from one man to the other, their bodies only inches apart.

Blood-spray dotted the guest book and freshly vacuumed carpet. I guess Thailand had one more job to do before they were truly finished with Maxine and her Montego Supremes.

I dropped to my knees and placed a hand on Peter's lifeless shell, shouting his name again and again. Frank grabbed my arm and pulled me away from the scene, maneuvering me past the crowd through the blossom-filled room toward the altar to a side door. One hand maintained an iron grip around my shoulder, the other balanced very near his gun. My shrieks of, "Where were you guys?" and "How could that happen?" remained unaddressed.

He did try to quiet me by interjecting that Peter was dead before he hit the ground and that he went real fast adding, "You're not in any danger, okay? You're fine. I've got you."

After that, I couldn't hear what he was saying, my own internal questions growing louder than his answers.

Before he got me through the door, I ground my heels in and grabbed the doorframe, trying to make him stop.

"Who was that other man, Frank?"

Without missing a beat, he put his arm around my waist moving me from the doorframe into the parking lot.

Felix managed to reach us as I was being ushered to my new vintage car waiting out back. I threw out my hand, he did the same, but Frank's forward motion kept us from connecting.

While I was being bullied into the car, Felix asked me what was going on but before I could answer, he turned to Frank.

"Hey, Francis, what the fuck? Don't you guys get paid enough? What the *fuck?*"

Frank never once looked at or attempted to answer Felix. Police escorts were already perched on their bikes in front of the Cad.

Felix made an unsuccessful attempt to negotiate his way to the passenger side, but cops had the car insulated and I was already inside.

Frank put his hand on the closed car window, his forehead practically touching the glass. "Julie…"

My attention shifted from fumbling for the keys Peter had given me to the man pressed against the glass.

"The other guy was Thongchai's second in command. He was a real bad man." Then he straightened up, hit the outside of the car door and yelled, "Get her out of here." Stepping away, he gestured to the motorcycle cops who started their engines.

Now sitting in the biggest front seat I'd ever been in, I turned the key, wrapped both shaking hands around the huge yet delicate steering wheel, and drove through the parking lot toward the hoopla on the street.

As my escorts and I slowly rolled through the alley along the side of the building, I could see media belching out of the side door where Peter and his assailant awaited transport to the morgue. Yes, it was a good day for the press.

I kept thinking how could something so heinous happen with all those police around? How could it? The answer I came up with was it couldn't. Peter had been set up. That's why we got to have a memorial service. They just set him up and waited. They didn't have to wait long. Maybe Frank was hoping to keep him alive and relocate him but saving the little fish wasn't as important as catching the big one. I understood Frank DiAngelo much better once I figured that out, and I didn't like him.

As I turned onto the boulevard, I wiped the tears from behind my glasses and glanced at the suitcase that I no longer had to share with anyone. I tried to convince myself that maybe this was some kind of twisted blessing, Peter dying when he did. I mean, this way, he wouldn't have to be relocated. He wouldn't have to learn to live without her. I would never know for sure. What I did know was that the suitcase was mine, the suitcase and the Cadillac and the music. How weird is that?

As the motorcycles and I accelerated to twenty then twenty-five, I watched Felix get smaller and smaller in the rear view mirror. I'd have to trust him. He'd have to trust me. I stroked the suitcase next to me on that grand front seat.

So now they were all dead, Maxine, her son, Peter, and Happy Man, all within weeks of one another. Interesting how things go sometimes. These people had been bound together so tightly for so long it almost seemed there was a metaphysical chokehold on all of them, inescapable, inextinguishable.

I thought how important it is to make sure people understand how you feel about them before one of you checks out. After digging around in my purse for a piece of paper, I found one. It was the blank page that had flown in my window the night of the fire.

With one hand, I layed it across the suitcase.

Finding a pen, I wrote down what I thought might make a good title for my impending book. "For The Record."

23

❖❖❖❖❖❖

So, this is the corner, 5th and Vanguard. That's the liquor store I was standing in front of, sucking on a pop and struggling with a feeling of foreboding that, as it turns out, was completely warranted. Bob's is under new management according to the sign on the door.

I'm sitting on the hood of my Saab. It's the nicest car in Munson's lot. I don't need two cars and the Cadillac is everything a girl could want.

I'm reporting what I remember of the events that led me here on a small recorder that I purchased a few days ago. I even bought a cell phone.

I've been thinking I might start the book off with a little poem, like, *Some are born to chase their muse, some born to run from it. And some are born to be the muse, despite their better judgment.*

Okay, I'm no poet, but I am a writer. Well, not so much a writer as a celebrity, but the fact that I know the difference between the two is not going to sully this for me. I won't let it.

Though the literary community continues to re-fuse me entrance into their private club, pop culture has embraced me as one of their own. No literary integrity needed for that club, just an audience, and right now I've got one.

Since arriving home from the hospital, it seems like every magazine and newspaper has either a picture of me or Maxine on the cover. Last week one of the tabloids had a split screen of Maxine in her hospital bed looking indescribably horrific and me in mine looking like The Mummy. I know I was in shock for three days but nobody remembers anybody taking a picture of me when I was laid up. The headline read "Death takes two – throws one back." This week, Variety ran their third front-page story on Maxine with my favorite headline to date, "Charred Chanteuse Chirps Ciao." And on it goes.

The Home Shopping Network is coming out with a line of Maxine Montego jewelry. These are pieces designed to look just like the real diamonds she gave away her last night on the air. Some gal called in to gloat that she had received one of the original pieces of jewelry from Maxine herself. I hope she's not dead. I hope I'm not. Surely Thailand needs to lay low for a while, at least in this neck of the woods. So I'm going to keep wearing my pretty ring until somebody cuts it off of me. Forget I said that.

VH1 is planning an in-studio concert featuring young pop icons of the day singing some of Maxine's songs with each kid's remembrances of when they first heard Maxine's work, how she shaped their work and so on. Now, I'm sure none of these kids has a clue who the hell Maxine was, but perhaps they will become fans at the suggestion of their press agents and management teams.

Some guy from PBS contacted me yesterday wanting to do a documentary about her. They want me to host it. Peter would've been a stronger contender for that job but, once again, Fortuna casts her freakish smile my way.

The jukebox at the coffeehouse has been stocked with some bargain bin vinyl of hers that people have dug up, and there's plenty of interest in re-releasing all of her work, separately and in box sets, as soon as we can put it together. Warner Brothers is falling over itself to do so in a hurry. Every beatnik baby from here to France wants to own something of Maxine Montego for their look-how-hip-I-really-am collections.

And, of course, a movie of Maxine's life is being talked about, a movie that I've been asked to work on as a consultant. God have mercy.

This and more discussed, planned, and some of it contracted in the last two weeks or so. Things move quickly in a disposable society. And I am somehow making money off of all of it, lots of money. There are moments when my good luck makes me very happy, other times, it makes me sick. But whatever serpents I'm dealing with in my own newly ignited pursuit of artistic expression, I'm genuinely glad that Maxine is finally getting her day in the sun.

The recognition she was denied in life is hers now that she's dead.

So, I guess I'm going to concentrate on getting on with it. Regroup a little. One thing celebrity has afforded me is access to as many bottles of pills as I deem necessary. Hello, old friends.

Now that I have some serious bread, I can buy anything I want. Hey, maybe I'll open a diner. I always kind of wanted to own a little diner. Maybe

I'll writer another novel. Who knows? Maybe my best work is yet to come.

Right now, I have to turn out a book about a woman I hardly knew. For a gal whose writing was on the wall she remained difficult to read. Felix is right, she's mythic; a mythic queen with a proclivity for getting herself wrapped up in some very serious shit, and that's only considering the stuff I know about. I could dig around for more but I won't do that to her. She lived with her secrets. She died with most of them. It doesn't have to be a terribly accurate biography. I certainly owe her more than I owe the publishing company and besides, they already gave me a butt-load of money. But I will make sure her music gets played. I made her a promise and I intend to keep it.

Anyway, I think I'm running out of tape so that's my story. I just want to add this final bit of advice.

If you want a promise that your muse will always be there for you, give it up. She doesn't come cheap and you don't have any entitlement to her time. She travels in shadows like a ghost. She'll crash your party then crawl out the bathroom window once you've gotten her a drink. She waits for no one. She's dangerous. And ultimately, she must be hunted down like the alluring, destructive criminal that she is.

HAPPY TO BE HERE
Words and Music by Maxine Montego

This is it – this is the brass ring
You were talking about it, rubbing your class ring
Stepped into a pile of glory
You smell successful
But your shoes know the whole story

Baby, look around you
They never thought you'd make it – somebody had to

So you finally got wise to the logic of compromise
Eat those words and bite that tongue
You're happy to be here
And if that's the way it goes
First your money then your clothes
Well, it's a con game, baby, but the joke's on them
'cause you're happy to be here

Step right up – pick your prizes
You paid for the balls, dear
Your pitching was priceless
Blushing you're nothing more than cotton candy
Those sticky fingers finally came in handy
Maybe the gloves you're wearing
Are only covering truths up
That were never worth sharing

Honey, no regrets
Take everything you can get
You get one shot, baby, now aim to win
And be happy to be here

They love you on your knees
Self-effacing as you please
The skin gets thicker when you crawl that long
You got this far
And you're happy to be here
Yeah, yeah
You bet

What was the magic combination
How does it feel to be a sensation
How'd you get those socialites
To underwrite each aberration
It wasn't destiny
Though you'll claim it was a little bit
It wasn't integrity
You just wanted it
You wanted it

So you beat the system and it beat you back
You can suffer that wisdom
From the driver's seat of your Cadillac
Now is not the time to reconsider every crime
C'est la vie, c'est la guerre
Say you're very happy to be here
Happy to be here
Happy to be here
Very happy
Very happy
Happy to be here

Watch for the second exciting installment in
THE JULIE PAGE SERIES...

"NIGHTHAWKS"

Coming Soon!

www.5thandvanguard.com